FINEST KIND

Lea Wait

Margaret K. McElderry Books
New York   London   Toronto   Sydney

Margaret K. McElderry Books
An imprint of Simon & Schuster Children's Publishing Division
1230 Avenue of the Americas, New York, New York 10020

Book design by Ann Zeak
The text for this book is set in Aldine401 BT.
Manufactured in the United States of America
10 9 8 7 6 5 4 3 2 1

Library of Congress Cataloging-in-Publication Data
Wait, Lea.
Finest kind / Lea Wait.—1st ed.
p. cm.
Summary: When his father's Boston bank fails in 1838, causing his family to relocate to a small Maine town, twelve-year-old Jake Webber works to prepare the family for the harsh winter while also keeping the existence of his disabled younger brother a secret.
ISBN-13: 978-1-4169-0952-1 (hardcover)
ISBN-10: 1-4169-0952-4
[1. Survival—Fiction. 2. Cerebral palsy—Fiction. 3. People with disabilities—Fiction. 4. Secrets—Fiction. 5. City and town life—Maine—Fiction. 6. Maine—History—1775–1865—Fiction.] I. Title.
PZ7.W1319Fin 2006   [Fic]—dc22   2005025422

FIRST
EDITION

FINEST KIND

Also by Lea Wait

For young readers

Stopping to Home
Seaward Born
Wintering Well

Margaret K. McElderry Books

For adults

Shadows at the Fair: An Antique Print Mystery
Shadows on the Coast of Maine: An Antique Print Mystery
Shadows on the Ivy: An Antique Print Mystery
Shadows at the Spring Show: An Antique Print Mystery

Scribner

For my grandchildren, Vanessa and Samantha Childs,
Taylor and Drew Gutschenritter, Aaron Wynne,
and my step-grandchildren, Kate and Addison Grant.

And, especially, for my first granddaughter, Tori Wait.

And for all children whose families have secrets.

With thanks to my editor, Sarah Sevier;
my husband, Robert Thomas;
and my friend, Kathleen Reed, M.D.,
all of whom read this manuscript and made valuable
suggestions that improved it.

❖ 1 ❖

September 11, 1838, Wiscasset, Maine

"We're almost there, Jake! Put down your book and look at your new hometown," Father called from the high front seat where he sat with the driver.

Jake tucked Nathaniel Hawthorne's *Twice-Told Tales* between two crates and stretched to look over the side of the open wagon packed with all their belongings. Mother rubbed her eyes and sat up too. She'd been dozing next to the nest of quilts and blankets she'd tucked around Frankie.

Six days had passed since they'd headed north from their home in Boston. Since then they'd seen little but rutted dirt roads, other horse- or ox-drawn wagons, an occasional river ferry, and a few small towns. Mr. Abbott, the teamster they'd hired to pack and drive their belongings, had stopped every few hours so he could harness new horses at an inn or way station. While he cared for the horses, the Webber family had stretched and eaten and relieved themselves. Other than that, Jake and Mother and Frankie had been trying to find comfortable positions in the back of the jouncing wagon, among the crates, barrels, chairs, and bedsteads.

Jake glanced at Frankie, who continued sleeping. Frankie had been his brother for six years, but he'd seen more of Frankie in the past days than he had ever before. At first he'd felt uncomfortable, watching Frankie's unfocused eyes and uncontrolled movements. Then he'd spent hours wondering how two brothers could be born so different. What if he'd been born like Frankie?

"It's a pretty little village," Mother said optimistically as they headed down a hill onto High Street, a short street lined with elegant homes ending at the Green, where a white church overlooked the town.

"That must be the Lincoln County Courthouse, next to the church," Father called down. "Cousin Ben told me Wiscasset was the center of Lincoln County."

If these few streets were the center of the county, Jake wondered what the rest of the area was like. Probably just more fields and woods and the occasional farmhouse, like they'd seen for the past many miles. Here there were no wide streets filled with elegant carriages. What kind of people lived in a place like this?

They had no choice. They would find out.

The wagon turned down the hill, onto Main Street, where there were more large white houses and inns. Other wagons and carts stood before two taverns, an inn, and several small stores. Jake saw an apothecary's sign, and a window displaying brightly colored cloth. Several boys were laughingly pouring water on each other's heads from a public pump. Three men were unloading a cart filled with firewood. A group of women carrying baskets chatted opposite them. Ahead, at the bottom of the hill, was a river. Maine was full of rivers; it seemed they'd crossed one every few hours since they'd left New Hampshire.

Jake didn't have time to see more before the wagon turned north. At first there were other grand houses along this side road, but as they drove farther from the center of town, the dwellings became smaller. They passed an old burying ground, and an occasional isolated farm.

Chickens squawked in the yards, and large barns were connected to small houses by a series of rooms. Fields of wheat or corn stretched on both sides of the road. Jake wondered if there were as many people in Wiscasset as there were chickens. He tightened his hold on the side of the wagon. What kind of life would this be? Would he ever have friends here like the boys at his school in Boston?

"We have to believe it'll be all right, Jake," said Mother, reaching out to touch his hand. "Cousin Ben has found us a place to live, and Father has a job. It will be different from Boston, but we'll be fine."

Jake nodded. He knew Mother was reassuring

herself as well. She'd cried when they'd left their home in Boston.

The road was narrower now. On the right they passed a white house attached to a heavy granite building. "That's the Lincoln County Jail," called back Mr. Abbott. "The jailer and his family live in the house."

Jake looked at the high granite walls. He hoped their new home was far away from that building and its occupants.

"Cousin Ben said our place is two miles past the jail," said Father. "We're almost home."

⚹ 2 ⚹

"You expect us to *live* in this hovel?" Mother asked, her voice rising. "In this wilderness?" Father kicked clods of dirt along the floor of wide pine boards and into the corner, and laid Frankie down on the cleaned spot. Frankie moaned, moved a little under his quilts, and then was still. "With only an outside pump for water and a fireplace for heat and cooking?"

For six days Father had been encouraging Mother to smile; their new life would be a new start. But this weather-beaten building meant to be their new home held out little hope.

Jake put down the crate of dishes he was carrying, left his book on top of the crate, and looked around. The inside of the small house was dark; the shutters on all three windows in the main room were closed. On the far side of the chimney was a second, even dingier, room that smelled of unemptied chamber pots and moldy straw.

Their three-story home in Boston had twelve

high-ceilinged rooms, including one floor of bed-
rooms just for the servants, and a pantry and large
kitchen below the first floor. That kitchen was larger
than these two rooms combined.

Since the Commonwealth Bank of Boston closed
in January and Father lost his job, raised voices had
become commonplace in that Boston home.

Jake didn't want to hear Mother and Father arguing
again. He moved toward the door.

Every morning for the past eight months he'd
watched Father leave to look for work. Every evening
Father had returned, weary and discouraged. First the
maids had left, and then the cook, and finally their two
carriage horses were gone, along with Adam, who
cared for them. Father told Jake he shouldn't plan to
return for the summer session of his private school.

Jake missed seeing his friends during the summer
and knew he would fall behind in his studies. But he
was twelve—almost a man. Too old to complain.

Then four weeks ago the letter had come from
Cousin Ben. There was work in Maine. Not in a bank,
but in a lumber mill in Wiscasset, if Father was interested
and "ready to dirty his hands," Cousin Ben had written.
Far north of Boston able-bodied men were still needed
despite the hard times people were calling the Panic.

Cousin Ben had promised to find them a place to
live if Father sent money ahead.

And here it was.

"There's no space here for the boys." Mother gestured at the room. "This house—if you can call it that—is dark and foul."

"Dirt can be scrubbed," Father said.

"How can I care for Frankie? He needs warmth, and a protected space."

"You'll manage. Women do," said Father. "I know this isn't easy. The house isn't what we expected. But for now it is what we have. We'll find a better home after I've earned some money."

Jake slipped out the door into the small yard where Mr. Abbott was unloading their furniture, crates of pots and pans, and barrels of clothing and bedding. Mother was right. This new home was worse than he had ever dreamed.

"Give me a hand?" Mr. Abbott asked.

Jake reached up to take one end of the large table they'd had in their Boston kitchen, and balanced it as Mr. Abbott lifted the other end off the wagon.

"You're small for your age, but you're strong," he said approvingly. Then he looked at the gray house. Shingles were missing, and the privy door hung open and crooked. The slanted roof on a lean-to led to a water barrel below it. Land where a barn had once stood was now overgrown with goldenrod and grasses. "This place is considerable different from your place in Boston."

"Yes."

Mr. Abbott looked straight at Jake. "Times are hard

now for lots of folks. But people make do. Times will get better. You and your parents are lucky to have each other."

Jake didn't feel lucky.

He heard his father's voice from inside the house. "Right now we have no choices! This is the way life is!"

Jake needed to get away; to separate himself from this place, and from his parents' arguing.

He ran down the rocky wagon path that led from the house to the road. Running came naturally, and felt good. He knew he was fast.

But after six days of sitting or lying in the back of the cramped wagon, Jake's muscles were stiff. He headed south, back toward Wiscasset, focusing on the ruts dug by wagon wheels in the stone-strewn earth. Running on the cobblestoned streets of Boston was no preparation for navigating this uneven dirt road.

He winced as he twisted his ankle in a small hole. He had to be more careful. Breaking his ankle would only complicate life more.

In Boston he'd run past men searching for work and families living in streets that smelled of horse and human waste. At least here no one was begging for food. Here there were just the tall dark spruce trees that bordered the road.

Jake slowed down but kept running. A small weather-beaten barn and an even smaller house were on his right. The house was low and unpainted and leaned a bit to the left. Scrawny chickens scratched in the dirt yard. Who would choose to live in such a place? For a moment Jake thought he heard a child crying. But when he stopped to listen, he only heard the wind and the shrill sounds of herring gulls who'd sighted food. Maybe the family who lived here had never known better. Or maybe, like his family, they had run out of choices.

Jake felt his muscles tightening with anger. Didn't Cousin Ben know Mother had always had the help of servants? After their cook had left, Mother had tried to use the stove in their Boston kitchen, but her bread had been dry and her broth salty. How would she manage with just a fireplace?

Where would they all sleep in the new house? How would Mother care for Frankie?

Why did Father have to lose his job?

Jake turned around. By now Father must have seen how impossible it was for them to stay here. Mr. Abbott was probably already reloading their belongings onto the wagon.

Jake looked over at the run-down house again. A figure was standing by a wide sugar maple at the side of the house. Jake blinked and looked again, but the man was gone. He must have imagined him.

Jake started back. His parents would be looking for him.

✗ 3 ✗

At the house—at *home*, Jake silently corrected himself—
the arguing had stopped. It was clear they were staying.

Father and Mr. Abbott had already unloaded most
of the wagon, and Mother was taking a broom to the
wood floor. At least boards were easier to sweep than
wool carpets.

As Jake came in, she frowned. "Where have you
been?"

Jake gestured outside.

"Now you're back, would you open the shutters so
we can get some light and fresh air into this place?"

Jake went to the nearest of the three windows. The
shutters were nailed tightly in place. Whoever had
closed them had made certain they wouldn't blow
open. Mother had already unpacked two crates of
kettles and pots for the kitchen and was scrubbing a
shelf on the wall where she could store them.

Frankie was still sleeping. He didn't seem to hear
the voices and confusion around him.

Jake walked out toward the wagon. "Where are our tools?" he asked. "The windows are nailed shut."

"Here, boy," said Mr. Abbott, tossing him a hammer and a small iron lever. "These will help you open the barrels and crates, too."

The nails came out easily enough. Jake found hooks on the inside wall and fastened the shutters open, pushing up the glass panes to let air in. The house needed all the light and air it could get.

Breezes filled the room. Mother sneezed as she swept a pile of dust off the highest shelf. "Now at least I can see what I'm doing."

Father and Mr. Abbott carried the headboard and footboard of Mother and Father's high bedstead to the small room in back of the fireplace and began setting up the bed.

"Where will I sleep?" Jake asked. "And Frankie?"

"You can have the loft space." Mother pointed to a sliding door that Jake hadn't noticed in the ceiling. "We'll put our ladder below it so you can climb up. It won't be like your room in Boston, but for now it will have to do."

Jake ached as he thought of his small blue bedroom in Boston. His bedstead and commode and washstand were on the wagon. They probably wouldn't fit in a loft. Most of the furniture they'd brought from Boston wouldn't fit in the new house. "And Frankie?"

"He needs to be warm, since he can't stomp about

like you can when the temperatures drop. He'll have to be in this room, near the fireplace."

"But—the fire?" Jake's mind quickly raced through all the problems of Frankie being close to a fire. Near where Mother would have to cook. Close to the door to the outside.

Frankie's eyes were now open; perhaps hearing the sound of his name had woken him.

"We'll have to watch him all the time. Even more than usual."

Jake looked at his brother. Frankie's legs were moving a little under the blankets that covered him. At first Jake had watched Frankie carefully, thinking his movements meant something. Now he knew Frankie's arms and legs often moved for no apparent reason.

He wondered when Mother had learned that.

"He must stay in this room; there's no other space. We'll have to hide him if anyone comes here," continued Mother.

In Boston, Frankie had been in a separate room, on the floor where the servants slept. How could they hide him in a house with only two rooms?

"It will be hard. But remember, we're newcomers here, Jake. No one knows about Frankie. Not even Cousin Ben. And we can't let anyone find out. You were young, but you remember what happened in Framingham."

"I remember."

Framingham was where they'd lived when Frankie was born, six years earlier. Father and Mother had taken him to doctors all over Massachusetts, but no one could cure a boy born crippled and a half-wit. People said he was that way because of the sins of his parents. After they knew about Frankie, neighbors crossed the street to avoid being seen with any of the Webber family.

"If we know someone is going to stop by, we can move him to the bedroom." Mother gestured toward the room where Father was putting the bed together. "But even then, his voice . . ."

Frankie never cried, but he did make strange noises sometimes. They were all used to the sounds, but strangers would not understand.

Jake looked at his brother. What could Mother and Father have done that was so horrible a sin?

Most of the time, Frankie lay in his blankets and stared vacantly at the room, but his fits were frightening. Frankie's back would arch and his body would twitch and tighten. If his body hit a hard surface, he could bruise or cut himself. He could knock down furniture or lighted candles. Doctors warned that he should never be left alone.

When Frankie was two the Webbers had moved to Boston, where no one knew them, and where their house had a small warm room lined with straw pallets for Frankie and Annie, the woman who cared for him. The pallets had to be replaced often, because they were often soiled, but even the servants were too embarrassed to tell about Frankie. No neighbors had learned their secret.

But two months ago Annie, the last of their servants, had left.

Mother had moved into the small closed third-floor room with Frankie, and Father had slept alone in the high bedstead. Mother could not cook when she was with Frankie, and she could not leave him alone. So Father had brought home bread and cheese or sometimes cooked meat or vegetables from a tavern.

Now Mother sat on the floor next to her youngest son and brushed Frankie's black hair back from his face. She looked from him to Jake and back. Both boys had straight black hair and dark eyes.

Father and Mr. Abbott entered the room. "The bedstead's together. Just have to bring in the mattress and the wardrobe, and that room will be set. Jake, you help Mr. Abbott bring your bed in. It's still on the wagon. Hannah, did you tell Jake about the loft space?"

"Yes."

"Good. There's a cellar for cold storage under the house too. The entrance is from the outside, but there's more space in this place than it looked at first. Jake, bring in the ladder too, so we can lift your bed up into the loft. You and I can manage from there. Mr. Abbott's got to make a pickup in Boothbay Harbor, and needs to be getting on. He'll change his team in Wiscasset."

Father took Mr. Abbott out toward the wagon.

Frankie's body began to jerk and twitch.

Mother tried to move Frankie away from the crates so he wouldn't injure himself, but his rigid body was hard to hold. Jake got on the floor to help her. The first time Jake had seen Frankie have a fit, he'd been scared. Now he just hoped the fit wouldn't last too long and that Frankie wouldn't hurt himself or anyone else. He knew what to expect, but he wondered if he would ever get used to seeing Frankie like this.

Frankie's eyelids fluttered. His drool covered Mother's hand, which was on his shoulder, and dripped onto the quilts. Jake reached out to hold Frankie's other shoulder down on the floor.

The spasm only lasted a minute or two. Jake could see Mother's hands relaxing as the seizure calmed. Then, suddenly, Frankie's body arched up. His left arm struck out and hit Jake's cheek. Jake moved back, knocking against a tall narrow crate leaning precariously on the wall in back of him. Mother pulled Frankie away as the crate teetered to the side. Jake reached out to steady it, but he was too late. The crate crashed onto the floor, narrowly missing them all. The sound of glass shattering filled the room.

4

Frankie always slept after one of his fits. Jake opened one of the crates, and Mother quickly unwrapped china she had packed in quilts. She then rolled the quilts to form a soft low wall around the spot on the floor where Frankie lay.

Father dismissed Mr. Abbott and helped Jake bring his bedroom furniture into the house and hoist it up into the loft.

The loft was hot in the early September sun. Jake opened the shutters on the single narrow window to let in fresh air. The loft was larger than he'd first thought; it was almost as large as the room below. But the ceiling slanted from the middle of the roof to the floor and at no point was it over six feet high. There was no space for his high walnut bedstead even in the center of the room.

Wooden racks for drying fruits and vegetables filled one corner, and a few pieces of dusty dried apple hung from a rope looped over a beam.

Jake piled the pieces of his bedstead in another corner and put his pallet on the floor near the window. Here it wasn't so bad; he could look out at the tops of trees. He had to be careful not to sit up too quickly, though, or he'd hit his head on the slanted ceiling.

He looked at the old slices of apple. They'd had nothing to eat since the beef stew in a tavern the night before. His stomach groaned as he thought about it.

Jake heard the creak and crack of nails being pulled away from a wooden crate downstairs. As he climbed down the ladder, he heard broken glass falling.

Father was standing in the corner of the main room, holding the frame of the carved mahogany mirror that had hung over their sitting room fireplace in Boston.

It had been packed in the crate Jake had knocked against when Frankie hit him. Shards of the mirror now covered the floor, reflecting the walls and ceiling of the room that was the center of their new life.

Mother picked up a long thin piece of the mirror. A drop of blood fell from her finger onto the floor. "At least the frame is not broken," she said. "When we're settled, we can get another mirror."

How long would it be before they again had a place to hang an elegant mirror?

⁎ 5 ⁎

"I'm really hungry," said Jake after he and Mother had finished cleaning the slivers of mirror from the floor. "Do we have anything to eat?"

Father stared at him blankly. "Eat?" Father looked as weary as Mother, and was dripping with sweat from moving furniture and crates. In the old days in Boston he would have hired men to do that work for him.

"Nathaniel, none of us have eaten since last night," Mother reminded him quietly.

"Cousin Ben said he'd be here this afternoon; he'll tell us what to do," said Father. They sat down in the chairs Father had arranged around their old kitchen table. The sale of their mahogany dining room table and chairs had helped pay for the move to Maine.

"When did you last see your cousin?" asked Jake.

"Not since I was younger than you," Father replied, relaxing a bit. "Ben's about my age. We were visiting our grandparents, outside Boston. My family lived in Framingham; Cousin Ben's lived in western

Massachusetts. About a year after that his family moved to the District of Maine. It was still part of Massachusetts then. I've heard from Ben over the years but haven't seen him in almost thirty years."

"Does he have any children my age?" Cousins who might be friends, Jake thought.

"Nope. Cousin Ben never married, so far as I know. Had a few lady friends, I heard, but never settled down."

"How does he manage on his own?" asked Mother. "In the city that would be possible. But here doesn't he need someone to do his cooking and cleaning and take care of his house?"

Until the last few months Mother had never done her own cooking and cleaning; now she was very conscious of all that was required to keep a home in order.

"He lives in a boarding house near the lumber mill," said Father.

"Then perhaps he has no idea what kind of a house is necessary for a family," said Mother. "When you tell him, he may know of another place for us."

Father looked at her directly and spoke softly. "We don't have money, Hannah. So we don't have choices."

"Surely there must be someplace more suitable than this," she said. "And before Cousin Ben gets here, you must help me move Frankie to our room, Nathaniel. You haven't told him about Frankie, have you?"

Father reached down and picked up Frankie. "No.

I didn't tell him about Frankie. What was there to say? And don't get your hopes high about the house. His letter said he'd gotten us the best place he could find."

If this was the best place, Jake thought, then what had other places been like? He thought of the house he'd seen that morning that was leaning on its foundations.

"We must ask him many things," Mother said as she picked up Frankie's quilts and followed Father into the bedroom. "We need to know where to get food, of course, and supplies, and about your job at the lumber mill, and who our neighbors are."

The wagon had left, and a dozen heavy crates were piled in the yard. Jake went outside and managed to lift one to his shoulder.

Their rooms in Boston had been decorated with fine furniture, draperies, china, silver, and brass. Treasured possessions like the mahogany-framed mirror that now was shattered. Many of Mother's favorite belongings had been sold, but she hadn't been able to part with everything. The brass candlesticks and oil lamp could be used here. But what would she do in this house with cut glass crystal and English porcelain? There was no space here for anything but necessities.

Jake found a place inside the house to put the crate down carefully and went to get another.

Maybe Cousin Ben would have a wagon and take them to an inn for dinner.

Jake stopped. No. They couldn't leave Frankie alone, and they couldn't take him out where people would see him.

Last night, when they'd stopped for a meal in Portland, Father and Mr. Abbott had taken turns sitting with Mother and Frankie in the wagon outside the tavern, bringing her food and soft bread pudding for Frankie. A woman couldn't sit alone in a wagon. It wouldn't be proper. Or safe.

Jake's stomach growled as he thought of that bread pudding flavored with maple and studded with raisins. Would Mother be able to bake puddings that good some day?

Maybe Cousin Ben would bring them some food. Beef stew. Or chowder. Wiscasset was near the coast.

Maybe here he could learn to fish! Then he could catch their dinner. For a moment Jake's spirits lifted. Then he wondered if Mother knew how to cook a fish.

❧ 6 ❧

"Cousin Ben!" Father strode out into their yard as a man almost twice his size, and with half as much hair on his head, came around the stand of pines shielding the wagon path to their house from the road. "I'd know you anywhere!"

Cousin Ben didn't have a wagon. He didn't even have a horse. And he wasn't carrying any bundles that might contain food.

Mother pushed past Jake and joined the men. Jake followed.

"This is my wife, Mrs. Webber, and my son, Jake," said Father. "We thank you for finding us this home, and the job at the mill."

Mother and Jake exchanged glances. They were grateful to Cousin Ben, of course, but was Father going to ask how soon they could move somewhere else?

"It's truly good to see you, Nathaniel, and to meet your family." Cousin Ben doffed his wide-brimmed hat in the direction of Mother and smiled at Jake.

"Welcome to the town of Wiscasset. You'll find this place a considerable change from Boston, for sure, but I hope a welcome one. Living here—it's the finest kind."

"Finest kind?" Jake repeated.

"That's Maine folks' way of saying something's the best of the best."

So far nothing here had seemed "the best of the best" to Jake.

"Won't you come in, Mr. Webber?" said Mother. "I am afraid I can't offer you anything more than water from the pump, but after you advise us where we can get groceries, we'll invite you back for a fine dinner."

"Please, call me Cousin Ben. We can't have two Mr. Webbers here!" Cousin Ben laughed as he followed Mother into the house.

Jake went to get the pitcher Mother had just unpacked, and he pumped water from the rusty pump in the yard. At first the water came slowly and foul, but finally it flowed clear and sweet. Jake poured them each a glass and sat down quietly. He didn't want to miss any of the conversation, but that wasn't a problem in this house. Every word could be heard in every room. No secret would stay hidden for long here.

"You wrote you'd want to start work as soon as you could, so I've told Mr. Stinson at the mill you'll be there tomorrow morning," said Cousin Ben.

Mother leaned back from the table a little.

"Of course; I do want to work," said Father. "Where is the mill?"

Cousin Ben hesitated. "A considerable distance," he admitted. "But there's an extra bed at the house where I board. I've already arranged for them to wait for payment till after your wages are paid."

Father's smile faded as Cousin Ben continued. "If that's fine with you, Cousin Nathaniel."

"Then . . . Nathaniel won't be able to come home nights?" asked Mother. She looked ashen, and the glass in her hand shook. "I didn't think of our being alone here without him."

"The mill is several hours' walk, on the southern side of Wiscasset," explained Cousin Ben. "I took the day off to greet you folks and make sure you were well settled."

"Do all men working at the mill live at the boarding house?" asked Father.

"Most do, unless they live close enough to walk, or have a horse."

"Could we find a home closer to the mill?" asked Mother.

"Nothing that would suit," said Cousin Ben. "Houses there are full, and there aren't many of them. And . . ." He paused. "Pardon my saying it, Mrs. Webber, but you would be more comfortable living in this area of Wiscasset. Most of those living south of town are rough, both the men and their women. It would be safer and more suitable for a lady such as yourself to be here."

Father looked at his wife with concern, and then at Cousin Ben. "We thought I'd be able to walk to work from our house, as I did in Boston."

"I didn't think to tell you. It's just the way it is here. Shall I tell Mr. Stinson you won't be coming to work at the mill, then?"

"No," said Father quickly. "I'll come. But perhaps after we get settled I can find employment closer to home."

"Indeed," agreed Cousin Ben. "But you may like the mill. Stinson's a good man to work for. We've got two saws, with box and shingle machines. And there's no end of work. Every shingle we make is shipped straight to the island of Cuba. They must be building fine homes there. And you'll have Saturday afternoons and Sundays off. You can see your family then."

Father nodded. "Of course. This is just another part of getting used to our new life."

Mother bit her lip.

"I hate to make my visit so short, but it's a distance to walk, and we'll want to get back to the boarding house before supper," said Cousin Ben, getting up from his chair. "Hours start early at the mill. Cousin Nathaniel, why don't you go ahead and gather some clothes. We'll walk back through the town. We can talk, and I can tell you the lay of the land."

"But, Cousin Ben," Jake blurted, "we have no food. What are we going to eat?"

Cousin Ben looked down at Jake and then at Father. "You brought nothing? Not even a few chickens?"

Mother shook her head. "We have no chickens. There was no need for them in Boston."

"Well, you probably haven't had time to explore yet, but there's a small orchard beyond the field in back of the house. Apples will be coming into season. And the old couple who lived here before you had a garden somewhere. The squash and pumpkins they left are yours too."

Mother's eyes looked glazed. "And milk, or meat? What are we to do for them?"

Cousin Ben hesitated. "Stacy's Store in town has groceries, but goods there are pricey, and it's a distance. There's a farm down the road. Ted Neal's place. They're good people. Jake can head back with us, and I can introduce him to them. Maybe they'd have some food to tide you over. They might even be able to sell you a chicken or two, so soon you'd have your own eggs."

Father looked at Jake. "We'll ask about chickens after I'm paid, but stopping at the farm today sounds like a good idea."

Father was really going to leave them alone in this unkempt house, with no food except a few vegetables in the garden. Squash! Jake hated squash.

Mother rose, blinking back tears. "Let me get you a basket, Jake. You'll need it if you can bring us back any food." She gestured for him to come closer as Father began pulling his clothes out of a barrel and putting some in a sack. She spoke softly, "Try to get some soft food for Frankie. Eggs would do. And milk, for tonight, and maybe bread. Or wheat, and salt, so I can make bread. While Frankie is sleeping, I'll gather wood for a fire, so if you're able to get food we can put together a meal when you return." She swallowed hard. "If there is no food, you'll have to look for those squash."

Jake nodded, but he couldn't help but make a face when she mentioned the squash.

"We can do this, Jake," Mother said. "It may only be for a short time." Mother held on to the back of a chair as if she might fall without its support.

Jake touched her arm. "I'll bring back something for us to eat," he promised. "And then I'll gather firewood. You just watch out for Frankie."

She smiled and let go of the chair. "Your father is going to work with men who live by their hands and backs and not by their learning. If he can change his life that much, and live in a boarding house, then you and I can find ourselves something to eat. We won't have him worrying about us, will we?"

Jake shook his head. He hadn't thought about what Father would do at the mill. Father had always worked in an office at the bank.

"Those are awfully fine shirts for millwork," Cousin Ben said to Father. "Haven't you any work clothes?"

"Where could I get some?" Father asked in a quiet voice.

"They've got ready-made clothing at Stacy's," advised Cousin Ben. "We can stop on the way and you can put them on account. John Stacy knows me. Get you a pair of pants and a shirt. That fine linen you've brought will only tear and get dirty. And wearing it might set off the boys at the mill. Don't want them figuring you think you're too good for Wiscasset."

Father nodded slightly. "I have a few dollars." He handed several coins to Jake. "Here. For food until I get back on Saturday. I'll take a little for the new clothes it seems I need."

"You'll fit in soon enough, Cousin," said Cousin Ben, slapping Father on his shoulder. "I remember you as a boy, climbing trees faster than any of the others, and leaving your books to run with the rest of us. You've been inside that city too long. You need to get back to the world of real men!"

Mother tried to smile.

"Hannah, take care." Father put his arms around Mother and whispered, "I'll be home soon." He moved toward the door, following Cousin Ben. "Jake here's almost a man. You'll not be alone."

"Come on then, the two of you. We've got to head out," said Cousin Ben.

Jake picked up the basket Mother had given him. It was the one their cook had taken with her when she went to the marketplace.

Wiscasset. His new life.

❖ 7 ❖

Jake followed Cousin Ben and his father as they walked toward Wiscasset. The road was already looking familiar.

"Is that where the Neals live?" asked Father. He pointed at the unpainted barn Jake had seen earlier. Now there were clothes drying on bushes near the house.

"No. Those people are not your sort," answered Cousin Ben. "Mrs. McCord stays to home caring for their young'uns; I've only met her once or twice. Ob McCord is a mariner on the coaster to Baltimore and Charleston."

"What's a coaster?" Jake asked. In Boston a coaster was a sled children played with in the snow.

"A ship that goes between two cities, carrying people and packages. There are coasters from Wiscasset to Portland and Boston, and even to southern ports like Charleston."

That sounded like a better way to travel than in the

back of a wagon. People sailed between ports, of course, but Jake had never heard the ships called coasters. "Are coasters for rich folks?" he asked.

"Moderately rich, in any case," Cousin Ben said, and laughed. "Lots of Mainers prefer the seas to the roads. But instead of rough roads, they have rough seas to contend with."

"Why aren't the McCords 'our sort'?" asked Jake.

"They're not what you'd call the tops of society." Cousin Ben shook his head as they walked on. "But the Neals—where we're going now—why, I've heard they're good folks. Have a boy about your age too, Jake."

A boy his age! Jake's spirits rose as he walked down the road with the men. "Do you know everyone in town, Cousin Ben?"

Cousin Ben laughed. "Pretty much. I've lived in Wiscasset a lot of years. I know the folks at the mill, of course, and most of the people in town. There's one church, so if you're God-fearing, that's where people are on Sunday. Some of the newer families in town I don't know, and I've given up keeping the names of all the children straight. But once you've lived here for a while, you'll know most folks too."

"I guess there are no secrets in Wiscasset," said Jake.

His father gave him a swift frown.

"Not likely," agreed Cousin Ben.

The Neals' white house was just ahead. A dozen

cows were grazing in a pasture in back of the house. As Jake looked at the cows, a large black dog galloped around the barn and stood, barking loudly at them. Jake moved to the side. Dogs in the streets of Boston were fierce if you got between them and what they'd found to eat.

The farmhouse door swung open, and a plump woman came toward them, her hair pinned up and her sleeves rolled as though she'd been washing or kneading bread.

"Can I help you?"

"Mrs. Neal," said Cousin Ben. "I'm Ben Webber, from over to the mill."

"Of course. I've seen you in church. What can I do for you, Mr. Webber?"

"My cousin, Nathaniel Webber, and his wife and boy, Jake here, moved into the old Crocker place today."

Mrs. Neal turned to them. "Welcome to you. Where do you folks come from?"

"Boston," said Father.

"And will you be farming?"

"I'll be working at the mill, like Ben," said Father.

"How old are you, Jake? Seems my Tom might be about your age."

"Twelve, ma'am," said Jake. "Thirteen in early January."

"Luck comes to a baby born close to the New Year,"

she declared. "But I suspect you all came for more than saying hello. Won't you come in? I see you've a basket, Jake."

The Neals' kitchen was large and warm, and smelled of bread baking and vegetable soup simmering on their large stove. Jake inhaled deeply.

"The Webbers being from Boston and all, they didn't think of bringing food with them, and we wondered if you and Mr. Neal could sell them some foodstuffs to last for a couple of days," said Cousin Ben.

"Sell! I wouldn't think of it," said Mrs. Neal. "You must be starved after your journey, and getting settled. Let me see what I can find."

"We don't want charity," said Jake. "I could help Tom with some chores, in return."

"You'll fit right in, then!" said Mrs. Neal approvingly. "That's just the way things are here. But I'd guess you have a few things to help your mother with now, especially with your father off to the mill. The food today will be a housewarming gift. No need to repay us except with friendship."

"Yes, ma'am," agreed Jake. The Neals' kitchen was almost as large as his family's whole house. Would their home ever be as clean and efficient as the one he was standing in now? "We all thank you."

"I'll plan to come down and welcome Mrs. Webber in person right soon," Mrs. Neal added. "Might not be easy for a Boston lady to adjust to country living."

"We're not set up for company just yet," put in Father. "You understand."

Mrs. Neal reached over and took the basket from Jake. "I'm not company; I'm a neighbor. And it happens I baked extra bread this morning." She put a large loaf in the basket. "Perhaps a few eggs would taste good after a long trip?" She added a dozen to the basket. "Jake, do you like corn?"

"Yes, ma'am." Corn was a lot better than squash!

"Go on out to the barn and find Tom. He'll show you where the corn is still good, and you pick as much as you'd like. Then come on back here and we'll get you set."

Jake ran out the door and over to the barn. What would Tom be like?

The barn was large and smelled of animals and hay. The Neals had cows and chickens, and an ox yoke hung on the wall. Maybe they had oxen as well. Jake dodged as a bird swooped low toward his head and then landed on a high beam.

"You never seen a barn swallow?" A brown-haired boy whose muscles and height made him look more fourteen than twelve was standing in one of the stalls. His face was dark from the sun, and his boots and trousers were splattered with muck. "Who are you anyway?" He pitched a fork-load of dung out of a stall and in Jake's direction.

"Jake Webber. My family just moved into the old

Crocker place down the road." He looked up at the swooping birds and ducked again as one flew close. "In Boston, birds didn't dive at me."

"Too bad for Boston," said Tom. "A barn's unlucky if it doesn't have barn swallows."

"We didn't have a barn. Only a stable."

"'Only a stable.' So you're one of those rich folks who don't need to get their hands dirty." Tom leaned on his pitchfork and looked at Jake. "What're you doing in my barn disturbing my barn swallows, Boston boy?"

Jake flushed. He'd never been called rich before, and today he felt poorer than he ever had before. But he refused to let this country boy intimidate him. "Your mother said you'd show me where to pick some corn. She said I could take some for our dinner."

"You ever picked corn before?"

"I can learn fast enough," said Jake. "And I know other things."

"What do you know?"

"I know the streets of Boston, and a little Latin, and I've history."

Tom shook his head and laughed. "Latin and streets of Boston aren't what we consider learning in the State of Maine."

"I can run," said Jake. Tom might not value books, but he looked as though he'd value speed.

"Bet a city boy can't run as fast as a Mainer," said

Tom, coming toward Jake. "Happens I'm the fastest runner in this district of Wiscasset."

"Some day we'll see," said Jake. He was aching to show Tom what he could do. But now was not the time. "Where's the corn?"

"We've tied most of it in sheaves already, but there're some stalks still standing," said Tom. "I'll show you where. And for now I won't tell the other boys you didn't know how to pick it. Not until we see if you can really run." He walked closer to Jake, and looked down at him. "How about meeting me Friday at twilight on the road north of your place? We can see just how fast you are."

Jake didn't hesitate. "How far north?"

"There's a small pond. The road next to it is straight."

"I'll be there."

The corn was harder to harvest than Jake had realized. His fingers were cut by the sharp dry stalks before he finished. He took twelve ears.

"Don't you know anything?" Tom said, tearing off a thirteenth for him. "Always pick thirteen ears, for luck. When we race, I don't want you saying I made you unlucky."

"I see Tom's shown you the corn," Mrs. Neal said when they got back to the house. "Your father and cousin already left, Jake. They seemed anxious to get going. At least in September they don't have to worry about night coming down on them. Dark afternoons will be here soon enough."

Jake nodded. He wished Father hadn't had to leave so quickly. But at least Mother and Father wouldn't argue for a few days. He added his corn to the basket. Now it held not only the eggs and bread but also a jar of pickles, a pie, and a mess of fresh string beans from the Neal garden. "I thought you and your ma might enjoy a bit of sweet and a taste of sour your first day in a new home," Mrs. Neal said. "Life is full of both. And there's a bit of tea and a little sugar wrapped in linen at the bottom of the basket, and some cheese I made last week."

Jake's empty stomach ached just looking at the food. "Thank you, Mrs. Neal. This is much appreciated. Remember, I said I could come back and help out, in return."

"You, help us!" Tom smirked. "Don't think we need to learn any Latin."

"Be nice, Tom," said his mother. "Jake'll learn Maine ways soon enough. Jake, you just take care of what needs to be done to home now. We're neighbors, and neighbors are there for each other, so if you need anything more, you stop in. Farm's been in my husband's family for over a hundred years now, and we're not going anyplace."

Jake hesitated. "You've already been so generous. But I saw cows out back. Would you have . . . a little milk?"

"Milk! That's for babies. Do city boys drink milk?" said Tom.

Jake was silent. He couldn't tell anyone about Frankie. "Mother's weary and her stomach's a bit upset after the journey. A bit of custard might help her."

"Nothing like custard to settle the stomach and the nerves," agreed Mrs. Neal. "Tom, get a pint from the back shed. And, Jake, you tell your mother I'll be by to visit as soon as she's ready for company."

"I'll tell her, Mrs. Neal. But she's real busy now."

"Winters are long here, and she's going to need friends. Besides, we're your closest neighbors, and I could do with having another woman nearby. With your father at the mill most of the week, I'd guess soon your ma'll be wanting a bit more company than you can provide."

"What about the family who live between our houses?" Jake kept thinking of that other house and barn.

"Your ma won't be getting much neighborliness from Mrs. McCord. You'll find that out soon enough. In the meantime, if you're needing anything, you come back here, Jake Webber."

Tom came in with a tin pint measure filled with milk, and his mother placed it carefully in the basket.

"You've got a lot to carry," she assessed. "Tom, why don't you walk with Jake?"

"I've not finished my chores, Ma," said Tom.

"I'll be fine," said Jake. Tom mustn't come! "My mother and I thank you both for everything. You've been very generous." He took the basket and started toward the door. "Tom, I'll see you Friday. At twilight."

⚹ 8 ⚹

By the time Jake got home, Mother had gathered a few broken branches and piled them on the hearth. Frankie was whimpering, and she was singing softly to him. "I had a little nut tree, Nothing would it bear, Save a silver nutmeg, And a golden pear . . ."

"What wonderful neighbors we have," she said as she sorted through the basket Jake had brought.

"Mrs. Neal seemed really nice. And Tom is about my age," shared Jake.

"Maybe you've found a friend," Mother suggested.

"Maybe," said Jake. He'd know more about Tom after their race Friday.

Mother handed him the pie. "Cut yourself a piece; I know you're starving. I'll soften a bit of the bread with the milk for Frankie. It's a warm day to think of fires now, and we'll have more strength once we've eaten."

Jake cut two pieces of blueberry pie, one for himself and one for Mother. While he was away she'd unpacked pewter dishes and tableware.

Mother broke small pieces of soft bread off the loaf. Frankie couldn't chew well, but he could swallow stewed foods, or softened bread. Mother tied a piece of muslin around his waist to hold him upright in a chair so he wouldn't choke.

Jake tried not to stuff the pie into his mouth, but it was hard. He was so hungry, and the pastry crumbled easily. Frankie must have been hungry too. He gurgled and drooled only slightly as Mother spooned the bread and milk into his mouth.

After Frankie had eaten, Mother turned to her piece of pie. "I'd heard there were wonderful tart blueberries like this in Maine. These were dried, so I suspect we've missed fresh for this year. But I'll try to make an apple pie after we get some flour. Mrs. Neal sent us some sugar, and I'll use the apples from the orchard Cousin Ben said was here."

"Mrs. Neal said she'd visit you, to welcome you to Wiscasset." Jake lowered his head as he saw the expression of panic on Mother's face. "I told her you had many things to organize, so you wouldn't have time for company soon."

"That was good, Jake. We must put off having visitors as long as we can. The only way to be sure no one knows about Frankie is to keep everyone away." Mother put her hand on Jake's. "This is a different world. I have to stay with Frankie. And with your father at the mill I'll have to depend on you for almost everything outside the house."

Jake's stomach tightened. In Boston he'd been responsible for his studies, for staying out of the way, and for being polite. He was twelve! How could anyone depend on him "for almost everything"? How could Mother even expect him to know what needed to be done?

He wanted to run away; to get away from the dank crowded house and all that was needed there. If only life were the way it had been before Father's job had disappeared.

Jake looked around. The room was still piled with crates and barrels and furniture.

"I can unpack the barrels, if you'd like. You can tell me where you'd like our things," said Jake. "What we can't use now can be stored in the lean-to or the loft." If he kept himself busy, then maybe he wouldn't have time to worry.

"First I'm going to look for curtains in those barrels so we can cover our windows. They'll protect our privacy a little."

Cool late afternoon breezes were beginning to blow through the open windows. The air smelled clean, and there was no one living close to them. Of what use would curtains be?

But they were important to Mother. Houses in Boston had curtained windows.

"Then I'll look for wood," said Jake. "We'll need to cook the corn tomorrow, and in case of rain we'll need dry wood on hand." There was a crate of tools, he remembered. "I'll find the ax." He'd never chopped wood before, but now there was no one else to do it. He'd learn how.

"I'll find our oil lamps," agreed Mother. "It will be light for another hour or two, but after dark I want to be able to see, should Frankie have another fit."

Jake stood in the doorway. "We're going to be all right, Mother. Somehow we're going to be all right." Maybe if he said the words loud enough, and often enough, then he'd begin to believe them himself.

❧ 9 ❧

Jake spent most of Friday chopping wood, fixing the door of the privy, and waiting for twilight. The time he was to meet Tom for their race.

It had been three days since they'd arrived in Wiscasset. Jake's hands were blistered from the ax, and his head ached from trying to think of what else needed to be done to help Mother. But he knew what he had to do that night.

He'd prove city boys could run as fast as Mainers. Maybe faster. Tom was taller than he was, so he had longer legs, but lightness could be an advantage too. Between chores Jake stretched to keep his muscles loose for the race.

"I'm going to meet Tom Neal. We're going to run a bit," he explained to Mother after dinner.

"Boys are amazing," she said, shaking her head. "I would think you'd be exhausted. You've been working hard all day. But I'm glad you've found a friend so quickly. Try to be home before dark, though. Maybe you should take a lantern."

Jake sensed that carrying a lantern would mark him as a coward who was afraid of the dark. "I'll be fine, Mother. I won't be late."

The pond wasn't far. Jake got there before Tom did, and looked carefully at the stretch of road they were to run. It was smoother and straighter than where he'd run earlier in the week. Wheel ruts were shallow. And there weren't as many rocks here.

Crickets were beginning to chirp, and bats flew low over the pond in search of flying insects. Jake paced and stretched.

He didn't have to wait long.

"You didn't chicken out," said Tom as he came up the road. "I thought maybe you'd decided to stay to home with your ma. Not many boys want to race me."

"I'm here."

"We start at this point." Tom picked up a stick and drew a line across the dirt road. "See the tall spruce a way's down?"

Jake looked in the direction Tom was pointing. "The one on the left, whose shadow crosses the road?" It looked about a quarter mile away.

"That's it. We race to the near side of the shadow and then back to this line. Understood?"

Jake nodded. "Understood."

"I'll be waiting for you, when you get back here," said Tom.

"Fair is fair. I'll wait for you likewise," Jake replied.

They stood at the starting line. "I'll count. We'll go on three," said Tom.

Jake got into position.

"One . . . two . . . three!" Both boys lunged forward, down the road. Jake felt the familiar stretch in his leg muscles and leaned forward as he ran. Tom was slightly ahead, but Jake didn't want to use all his speed at the beginning. As long as he stayed close enough to Tom so he could catch him, he'd be all right, and if he could push Tom to use most of his energy in the first half of the race, he'd be in a good position to win.

Jake watched the road, carefully avoiding stones and holes and a few fallen branches. Tom remained ahead, but not far.

They were about halfway to the turning point. Jake was still running at a comfortable pace, but Tom was now a few feet farther ahead. Jake saved his strength and paced his breath to his strides. He'd speed up after they'd reached the halfway mark.

Tom reached the spruce shadow first, and grinned triumphantly at Jake as he headed back to the finish line.

Jake made his turn and picked up the pace. There was still a quarter mile to go, but he wouldn't let Tom get so far ahead that he couldn't be caught. Gradually Jake increased the length of his strides, and his legs and arms fell into a comfortable rhythm.

Tom was fifteen feet ahead of him. Then fourteen feet. Tom wasn't speeding up; he was running at the same pace he had from the start.

Jake pushed himself further. Thirteen feet apart. Twelve. Eleven. Ten.

Tom heard Jake and lost a few seconds looking back to see how close he was.

Nine feet. Eight feet.

Jake could see the finish line ahead. They were both breathing heavily. Tom had picked up his pace but clearly had reached his limit. Jake forced himself to go faster.

Seven feet. Six. Five. Now only a little over an arm's length separated them.

Jake slipped slightly on a stone he hadn't seen in the dimming light, and fell back a foot. Then he summoned every part of his body to perform, and sprinted ahead.

As they passed the finish line, Jake was only inches ahead of Tom. But he was ahead.

They both continued a few paces and then Tom collapsed on the road. Jake bent over, hands on his hips, breathing loudly. They were both sweating and struggling for breath.

Jake spoke first. "You're a fine runner, Tom. I only

beat you by a step or two." He had done it. He'd proved to Tom that he had some worth, even if he didn't know about barn swallows and picking corn. He waited confidently for Tom to congratulate him.

"You didn't beat me," said Tom belligerently. "No one beats me. You must have turned before the spruce shadow."

"I didn't!"

"This won't be our last race," said Tom, getting to his feet. "No Boston boy is going to beat me." He turned and headed down the road toward home.

Jake stood, still catching his breath. Clearly the race had been about more than who was fastest.

❧ 10 ❧

Father returned late Saturday afternoon carrying a large basket on each arm and a sack over his shoulder. His hands were blistered, his back was aching, and he was exhausted. But he'd brought wheat flour, a little beef and pork, two loaves of bread, and a dozen plums. Best of all, he'd brought four clucking chickens.

"Our own eggs!" said Mother with relief.

"Just watch out for this rooster." Father grinned as he opened the second basket. "He's a feisty one. Been trying to nip me through the basket all the way from town." The three hens that had been in the first basket plumped their ruffled feathers and ran about the yard, glad to be freed. The rooster shook himself and surveyed his new realm.

"What do we do with them?" Jake asked. He reached out to touch one of the hens, but she skittered toward the privy. "Won't they run away if they're not penned?"

Mother chased one of the chickens from the doorway of the house.

"I'm told they'll stay close to where you leave food and water," said Father. "They'll eat grasses this time of year, but we'll need to get them corn for winter."

"Some of last year's cornstalks were left in the back of the garden," Jake volunteered. "I've seen a few ears of corn there, but the kernels are very dry. I'll pick them, in case the chickens don't care." How much did chickens eat? "Next year we'll grow our own corn," he added with confidence. If Tom Neal's family could do it, so could they.

Would they still be in this place in a year?

"How was it, working in the mill?" Mother asked.

"I managed," Father said quietly. "Work days are twelve hours long, and sleeping in a room with ten men is not easy, especially when you're used to better company." He hugged Mother again and squeezed Jake's shoulder. "I'm glad to be home."

"You were missed," said Mother. "It looks as though you did without some soap and water when you were away."

Father laughed. "Working in a mill is not a way to keep clean. I bought soap in Wiscasset, and what I want even more than a soft bed is a scrubbing. At least here we can heat water and I can feel clean for a day."

While Mother heated water, Father showed her the heavy work clothes he'd bought. They already needed stitching as well as cleaning.

"The apples in our orchard are still green and sour,

Father. But there are two kinds of squash in the garden, and pumpkins and cabbages," Jake reported.

"I see you and your Mother covered the windows with curtains. But where did you put the rest of the furniture?" asked Father. "This room looks more spacious than when I left."

"I stored some of the furniture in the lean-to and some in the loft."

Father inspected Frankie's corner, where Mother had arranged pallets on the floor and walls. The rest of the room served as kitchen, dining room, and living room.

"Looks as though you've made a safe place for Frankie," Father said approvingly, looking down at his youngest son.

"I don't know what we'll do should someone stop to visit," Mother admitted. "But the nights are already getting cooler, and Frankie has to be in the room with a fireplace." She'd placed an elegant three-sectioned carved mahogany parlor screen so it partially blocked Frankie's corner, but nothing could completely hide the wall of pallets.

Father hugged Mother. "No one will be visiting us this far out in the country. Frankie's space looks fine. You've both done well. I shouldn't have worried. The house is beginning to seem like home." He looked at the iron kettle hanging from the crane in the fireplace, and the pot on the grate heating water. "When I left I wasn't sure you could make a fire, much less cook, in this place. I shouldn't have worried."

Mother and Jake exchanged looks. They wouldn't tell Father how long it had taken them to find and chop the wood, and then to get a fire started that burned well.

Father slept in his own bed Saturday night, adding that he wasn't sure he could ever drag himself out of it again. Mother slept on her pallet near Frankie.

Sunday afternoon while Mother finished mending a seam on one of her husband's shirts, Father and Jake sat on the doorstep in the sun. Father had to leave soon to get back to the boarding house before night.

"How is your mother managing?" asked Father quietly. "Truly."

"She's fine," said Jake. There was nothing Father could do when he wasn't there, and his worrying wouldn't solve any problems. "She's tired, as you are. And she's scared someone will find out about Frankie."

"What do you need most?" asked Father. "What shall I bring next week, if I can."

"More flour for bread," said Jake seriously. "Meat. Or fish. And oil for the lamp. Mother is afraid in the night, and leaves the lamp burning."

Father put his head down on his hands for a moment and then looked up at his son, who until now had never needed to think about flour or whale oil.

"You must be my eyes while I'm gone, Jake. If your mother is struggling, then I need to know."

Jake nodded but said nothing. Of course Mother was struggling. They all were. Why hadn't Father been able to find a job closer to home, so he could take responsibility for his family? They'd been in Maine less than a week and Jake felt as though they'd been there a year.

That night Mother, Frankie, and Jake shared a supper of squash roasted in the fireplace. Jake's mind was full of concerns. What would they eat this week? Where would he find more dry firewood for the winter? Would he ever find a friend in this place? When would he next see Tom—and what would happen when he did?

"I'm going to explore," he told Mother after he'd pumped some water and helped her heat it so she could wash Frankie and some of his clouts. Jake was restless, and he needed to think.

He walked past the garden into what had once been a pasture and was now high with end-of-summer grasses. Birds were gathering to fly south, and orange and black butterflies were searching milkweed and the last flowers of the season. Jake stopped and listened.

The field hummed with a quiet trill. Then the air filled with thousands of long-bodied blue and green dragonflies. The insects flew in straight lines, turning abruptly when they sensed anything near them.

Jake walked into the field and lifted his arms. The dragonflies approached him, then turned at right angles and headed in other directions. They never touched him or each other.

He'd never seen anything like this in Boston.

As he stood, hypnotized by the sight, he saw a girl standing among the trees on the south side of the clearing.

How long had she been there?

Slowly he walked toward her. She was shorter than he was, but perhaps as old. Her dirty flour-smudged gray apron and bare feet blended with the shadowed trees. A long untidy brown braid fell across her shoulder. As Jake got closer, he saw two small children standing slightly in back of her, almost hidden by tall grasses, dying Queen Anne's lace, and goldenrod.

She gestured to them to follow her, and all three walked out into the field, as though to greet him. Holding out her arms to the dragonflies as Jake had done, she turned around in a slow dance. "Come and see them," she called softly to the boy and girl. "The fairies have come to bless us before they disappear for the winter."

The little boy ran into the field, trying to touch the dragonflies, but they were faster than he was. The young girl just stood and watched, her fingers in her mouth and her large gray eyes wide open.

"Who are you?" Jake asked the older girl.

"Nabby. These are Violet and Zeke."

"Where did you come from?"

"Through the woods. I wanted to get some fresh air before night, and I can never leave without the children."

"You live near?"

"In the house next to yours. I heard you and your ma came from Boston, and your pa is working over to the mill."

"How do you know that?"

Nabby smiled and shrugged. "Everyone knows. Even when there are secrets, in Wiscasset everyone knows."

Jake looked at her. Could she know about Frankie? Did everyone know about Frankie?

"Have you secrets you don't want known?"

"Most families do, I think," said Jake.

"Yes," said Nabby. "Most do."

Nabby reached down to take Violet's fingers out of her mouth. As she moved, the dragonflies surrounded her, shining like beams of blue and green light. They did look like fairies.

"Zeke! Come back," she called to the boy who was running in circles amidst the insects. "The fairies must be on their way, and so must we." The boy ran over to her, smiling, despite his dirty feet and torn shirt.

"They are truly fairies, ain't they, Nabby?" he said, grinning.

"More than any other beings I've seen," she agreed. "Granny McPherson told me, and she knows the ways of creatures."

Zeke nodded seriously. "She does."

"Is Granny McPherson your grandmother?" Jake asked.

"She's a friend," said Nabby. "We must get back now." She turned, and took the children's hands. "I've heard your name is Jake."

"Yes," said Jake, wondering where she had heard so much. Perhaps from Tom? "Will I see you again?"

"Our homes are not far from each other," said Nabby.

The three figures disappeared into the woods, leaving Jake in the meadow. He turned and looked. The dragonflies were gone. For a moment he thought he saw another figure in the woods. A man, standing in the shadows near where Nabby and the children had disappeared.

He took a step toward the figure, but the man vanished into the pine woods.

Jake shook his head. The darkness was gathering, and his eyes must have tricked him again. He was alone.

It was late the next week before Jake got back to the Neals' farm. Their barnyard was quiet except for the clucking of chickens, a noise he was becoming accustomed to. Jake had run to the farm, and now he paused a moment to catch his breath. Not even the large dog was in sight. Maybe no one was home. Jake rapped on the kitchen door.

Mrs. Neal answered almost immediately. "Jake! It's good to see you again. How are you and your mother managing? I saw your father walking home Saturday and then going back to the mill Sunday." She shooed Jake inside. "It must seem like a long time between his visits. I saw he was carrying two baskets and a sack."

Nabby had been right. There were no secrets in Wiscasset.

"He brought us a rooster and three hens, for eggs," said Jake.

"And a good start that will be. More work for you but a blessing for your mother and her cooking," Mrs.

Neal said. "You'll be enjoying that, too, I'll wager."

"We have no eggs yet, but the chickens should be settling down soon."

"Chickens can be tricky about where they hide their eggs. Look behind loose boards or under your shed and beneath the leaves of large plants. Finding eggs will be easier in the winter, when the hens are in your chicken house."

Chicken house! One more thing to do. "Mother sends her regards, and her thanks for all the food. She's not yet prepared to send anything in kind, but I came to see if I could help out, in return. Now that we're more organized."

"There's no work that needs helping with this moment, although I thank you for stopping. Mr. Neal is helping Owen Williams hay his field this afternoon. Tom took our dog, Chester, and went down to the Sheepscot to find oyster shells for the chickens."

"Oyster shells for chickens?" blurted Jake.

"You'll find they're much better than mussel or clam shells," said Mrs. Neal. "Crush them up and the chickens will eat them. Helps them digest their grains, and makes their eggshells harder."

Jake listened carefully, but oyster shells for chickens? He'd eaten oyster pies and oyster stew in restaurants in Boston. He'd even heard of crushing oyster shells to use them in plaster.

In Boston he'd taken restaurants and vegetable

markets and pocket change for granted. Here in Maine they took for granted that everyone knew how to care for chickens.

"Why don't you find Tom? You could gather shells for your own chickens." Mrs. Neal handed Jake a canvas sack. "I'll get you a knife, too. Perhaps you'll also find enough live oysters for suppers at both our houses."

Mother would be pleased if he brought home oysters for dinner! "How do I get to the river?" Jake asked, wondering what he would use the knife for. Opening the oysters? He'd watch Tom.

Mrs. Neal opened the door and pointed across the road. "See that stand of birches? Just to the left of the trees there's a path. Follow it a quarter mile or so and you'll come to the shore of the Sheepscot. Should be pretty close to low tide now, and that's the best time to find oysters, live or dead. Tom's there on the shore somewhere."

"Thank you, ma'am," said Jake.

The odor of pine was strong on the narrow path, and mosses crunched under Jake's feet. At first the woods seemed quiet, but then he began to hear birds everywhere. Crows and blue jays argued with each other loudly. Bright yellow goldfinches twittered and flew from branch to branch. Chickadees seemed to follow him as he walked. Sometimes a gray squirrel or a chipmunk ran ahead of him on the path, or a small red squirrel leaped from one branch to another far above his head.

Beyond the woods was an open area that had once been lumbered, and then farmed. The path was harder to follow there, but Jake could see a trail where high wild grasses had been tramped down. The breezes smelled of salt water. He was getting closer to the Sheepscot River.

Jagged pine trees shaped by winter winds grew on the land above the river. Their roots were anchored by piles of rocks. Some of the rocks had been uncovered by storm tides, and some thrown there by farmers clearing their land. The rocks now bordered the river at high tide and divided dry land from the sea grasses, seaweeds, and mudflats below.

Even at low tide Boston Harbor was never exposed like this. The Sheepscot River was far away, across a sea of dark mud.

Jake didn't see any oysters. Did they live in the mud, as clams did? Or perhaps on the rocks or under the seaweed that kept the rocks damp even at low tide?

Tom would know, although Jake would have to show his ignorance again if he asked Tom for help. He'd hoped to find Tom immediately, and then just copy what he was doing. But there was no one in sight.

Jake left his sack and knife under the trees and climbed down to the high-tide mark. Maybe if he walked out onto the mud? He took off his boots, rolled up his trousers, and took a few steps across the slippery rockweed and kelp.

The dark mud was squishy between his toes and had a dank, salty smell. One step, then another, and then his right foot completely disappeared into the mud. Before he could pull it out, his left foot sank too. When he pulled his right foot out, it left the mud with a slurpy sucking sound. He could feel small rocks and shells cutting the left foot that was still sinking.

Jake tried to step back toward the sea grasses that bordered the mudflats, hoping to find a shallow spot, but as he yanked his left foot to loosen it, he teetered, lost his balance, and sat down in the mud. Hard. Then he heard loud barking and laughter.

"Look at the city boy playing in our mudflats!"

Another voice laughed louder. "Maybe he's trying to swim!"

"Maybe he thought the flats were frozen and he could skate on them!"

"Or run!"

"Trapped in Maine mud, Boston boy?"

Jake tried to turn toward the voices. With every movement he sank farther into the black unforgiving mud.

Tom Neal and a younger, heavier boy were standing on the rocks not far above him, grinning. Chester was wagging his tail wildly and barking loudly as he raced from one part of the rocky shore to another.

"Hey, Jake!" Tom called. "This looks like my mother's sack and knife on the rocks. You steal them from her?"

"I didn't steal anything! I'm looking for oysters. Your mother said you'd be here." Jake tried to reply civilly, but every time he tried to push himself up, he sank deeper in the mud. His face turned red with embarrassment. Now Tom would have another story to tell about how Jake didn't know Maine ways. *There must be a way to get out of this mud!* Jake struggled to stand, and sank farther. "I'm stuck!"

The boys laughed again, louder this time. "Looking for oysters? Maybe in Boston they grow in the mud!"

"I give up. I need help!"

"Looks that way," agreed Tom. "Wonder how deep the mud is? What do you think, Ed?"

Jake sank a little lower with every word.

"If we don't help him, he might be gone forever," said Ed with a grin. "I guess we should be Good Samaritans."

"Maybe Jake is reciting his Latin and doesn't want to be disturbed by us ignorant country boys," said Tom.

Chester barked his agreement.

"His ma is going to be really mad when she sees how dirty his clothes are," Ed pointed out.

"But he isn't *totally* covered by mud yet," said Tom. "Maybe we should wait until his shoulders and head are under too."

"PLEASE!" With every movement Jake made to get up, his arms and legs sank a bit farther. There was nothing to pull himself up with, or to balance on. He was pretty sure he wouldn't sink totally under . . . but the thought of the tide coming in was scary. How deep *was* the mud? He needed to get out. Now.

"Why should we help you?" Tom called.

"So you can have a chance to beat me the next time we race!" answered Jake.

This time Tom's face reddened. He must not have told Ed that Jake had bested him.

"Tom's the best runner here," said Ed. "He'll beat you, easy."

"We'll see," said Jake. "You can't be the best if you have no competition."

"Guess we don't need any dead bodies in the river," Tom said. "It would stink up the place. We'd better help him."

Tom and Ed climbed down the rocks toward Jake, and Chester happily followed, stopping at the edge of the mud. Tom walked a few yards along the shore through the deep grasses. He picked up a long gray sea-smoothed branch, headed back to a spot where the land was still solid, and stretched the driftwood toward Jake. "You hang on to the end, and we'll drag you out."

Jake took a deep breath, hoping this would work. He needed Tom's help, even if that meant listening to his taunts. Jake stretched and wriggled, and finally got one of his hands around the driftwood branch.

Tom pulled and pulled, but Jake didn't move. "Ed, you help too. Jake may be skinny, but he's as heavy as a whale."

Ed put his arms around Tom's waist, and they pulled with both of their weights. Chester tried to help too, pulling Ed's sweater as though they were all playing at tug of war.

Jake wiggled more, managing to increase the amount of mud covering him.

"Don't fight the mud," Tom advised, as sweat poured down his face. "Lift yourself slowly out of it."

Gradually Jake's mud-coated body began to emerge from the flats. Slowly Jake got closer to Tom and Ed, and to solid land.

Tom stopped pulling. "Here," he said, tossing the driftwood to Jake. "Use this to balance yourself, and see if you can stand up. The mud shouldn't be as deep where you are now."

Jake stuck the stick into the mud. Tom was right. He could pull himself up. Using the driftwood for balance he carefully walked the few steps left to the high grasses. Safe! "Thanks! I thought I'd be in that mud forever!"

Chester, disappointed the game was over, was sniffing a tide pool farther up on the ledges.

"If you're stupid enough to walk on the flats again,

stay in areas outside the channel line," said Tom. "You'd still sink up to your ankles, but you'd probably survive."

Jake nodded. "I'll remember." He turned to the other boy. "Hello, Ed. Pleased to meet you. And thank you!"

"Welcome to Wiscasset," said Ed. He was shorter than Tom, but his added weight had no doubt helped provide the force to help Jake emerge from the mud. "My father's the schoolmaster. Shall I tell my father he'll have a new boy in class for the winter term?"

"Do you think the genius is going to attend classes with us foolish country boys?" asked Tom.

Jake ignored Tom and answered Ed. "Tell your father I hope to attend his school." Jake tried to rub the drying mud off his trousers and legs. Perhaps he'd been foolish to think Tom would be his friend, but Tom *had* pulled him out of the mud. And if Ed's father was the schoolmaster, he had better be polite. "When does the term start?"

"Just before Thanksgiving. Stop in to see Pa, and he'll tell you what supplies you'll need," said Ed.

"No school until late November?" asked Jake. How much did this school cost? And what supplies were needed? Could he use the books he'd taken to classes in Boston? He had no money for others.

"Don't you know anything? No one's free for lessons until the harvest is in, the cider is made, and the butchering is done for the winter," said Tom. "Then we have classes until we're needed for sugaring off, in March."

"Is it different in Boston?" asked Ed.

"Yes," said Jake. He didn't want to talk about the differences between private classes and public schools, city schools and country schools. Boston schools didn't have to wait to start until the butchering was done for the season. "Tom, your mother said you were looking for oyster shells, and maybe oysters."

"I've already filled my sack," said Tom. "Then I saw Ed and went to talk with him. That was before we saw a beached Boston whale."

"I was playing with Annie," said Ed. "She's my sister, who's five. Margaret's the baby. She's two. I get tired just having girls around, so I left them with Mother. Do you have a sister?"

"No," said Jake, hoping Ed wouldn't ask if he had a brother.

"You're lucky. Little sisters are the worst. They follow you around and always want to do what you do. And they're mean, too! Annie took my sea stone collection and buried it where I can't find it, just because I wouldn't play dolls with her. I hope Ma's next baby is a boy."

"Good luck!" said Jake. "Can you tell me where to find oysters?"

"Oyster shells get caught between the sea grasses,

where the tide has washed them in, or lie on the rocks, where gulls have dropped them," said Ed.

"What do you want to help him for?" asked Tom, turning his back and starting up the rocks. "Let him figure it out himself."

"And live oysters?" asked Jake.

Ed shifted his weight from one foot to the other and glanced at Tom before he answered. "They grow underneath rockweed, on rocks and logs. You have to cut them off. Seaweed keeps them damp at low tide, so they don't die."

"Come on, Ed," said Tom. "We have to take my shells back to the barn to grind them." He paused. "And we'll take this bag and knife back to Ma, just in case she's missing them." He turned and ran back into the woods. Chester bounded after him. Ed took one more look at Jake, shrugged his shoulders, and followed.

Jake felt very wet, very dirty, and very foolish. And he had no oysters for dinner.

This time.

❈ 12 ❈

Jake found two eggs under the leaves of a large prickly thistle plant, and three in a corner of the lean-to, where a hen had squeezed between two loose boards. They made a scant, but tasty, supper. *Finest kind,* Jake thought, remembering the phrase Cousin Ben had used. After supper he nailed the loose board on the lean-to and made a good start on building a henhouse out of boards pried from the crates they'd brought from Boston.

Night fell earlier and earlier each day, and there wasn't light enough to finish the henhouse that evening.

He'd washed the mud off as best he could when he'd returned home, but his hands, already cut from the broken shells in the mud, were now also swollen with thistle prickles and one badly aimed hammer blow. Mother sat at the table in the light of the oil lamp, sewing a patch on her petticoat. It had caught on the pump handle.

"Soaking in warm water will help those hands," she said, seeing him wince as he picked up his copy of *Twice-Told Tales* from the sideboard. "There's water left in the kettle."

Jake poured some of the water into the small basin Mother used for rinsing off tableware, and put his hands in. The cuts stung.

"You've done so much today. And I've managed to wash some clothes." Frankie's clean clothes were hanging on ropes stretched across the room. "Tomorrow I'll see if I can get the mud off yours."

Jake nodded. He'd left his muddy clothes outside to dry on the low limb of a tree.

"I saw the chicken house you built. Using the crates for wood was a good idea."

"There's a lot more to do," said Jake, flexing his fingers and gently rubbing spots that were still dirty. "Tomorrow I'm going back to the river to find oyster shells for the chickens. And, I hope, some oysters for us to eat."

Mother smiled. "What would Frankie and I do without you, Jake?"

Jake was glad Mother was pleased with what he'd done. But he wished Father could be home more often, and that they could depend on him, too. He wished he had time to walk in the woods, or read. He longed for one day of freedom, when he didn't have chores that kept him busy from first light to last.

The next morning while the chickens were exploring their new house, Jake took a knife and a sack and again headed for the Sheepscot. He started toward the Neals' farm to find the way he'd followed yesterday, but was relieved to see another path leading in the direction of the river. A closer path meant a shorter walk. And today he didn't want to run into Tom and hear his insults.

The tide was about halfway out. Or was it halfway back, Jake wondered. He'd have to learn about tides, too. All he cared about now was that the rocks, tall grasses, and seaweed above the mud line were exposed.

He carefully made his way down the rocks and walked through the grasses. Sure enough, when he looked carefully, he found broken oyster shells caught in the high sea grasses, just as Ed had said. More were half-buried in the shallow mud. He rinsed those that were muddy in a tide pool between the rocks.

And that was where he found his first live oyster, attached to the side of the tide pool, under a curtain of rockweed.

He carefully pried the oyster up, and then cut the few threads that attached it to the rock. He put the live oyster on top of the shells in his sack, and then covered it with rockweed to keep it moist and alive.

After he'd found one oyster and knew where to look, he saw others. Some were only two inches long.

He left those to grow. But others were six or seven inches long, and he happily harvested those from under the rockweed, mermaid's hair, and kelp that hid them. By midmorning he'd filled his bag and headed up over the rocks toward home.

❧ 13 ❧

That Saturday afternoon Father arrived bringing wheat flour, dried corn and beans, salt pork, and whale oil.

"Salt pork!" said Mother. "What can I do with that?"

"All the men from the mill were buying it at the grocer's," said Father. "It's said to give baked beans good flavor."

Mother made a face. "It will flavor soups, and I'll try it with the dried beans, but next time could you buy us beef instead?"

"I bought what we can afford," replied Father as he walked to the fire to heat water for washing up.

"You're limping!" said Mother. "What happened?"

"It's just a bruise," replied Father.

Mother looked at him, shook her head, and went to tend to Frankie.

Everyone was more relaxed later as they dined on baked oysters, eggs, and fresh bread Mother had made. And roasted squash, of course.

"Millwork is hard. The saws run day and night," said Father as he sat at the table after supper. "I'm earning wages, true, but I'm not used to moving heavy logs and boards and piling up shingles." The blisters Jake had noticed on Father's hands the week before were becoming calluses, and Father, never a large man, had lost weight. "I worry about the three of you here alone, but you seem to be managing well."

Jake and Mother looked at each other. Neither mentioned the days they were hungry and exhausted.

After supper Father admired the chicken house, and the two flat rocks Jake was using to grind oyster shells for the chickens.

"With only four chickens we won't need too many shells," Jake explained. "But if we have a sack of ground shells for the winter, I won't have to be looking for oysters under the ice in December." He hesitated. "When the grasses are covered with snow, we'll need more corn and wheat or oats for the chickens."

Father nodded, but clearly his mind was not on chickens. He went to sit with Mother on the granite step outside the house.

"How is Frankie?" he asked her.

"The same," said Mother. "Good days and bad. It's hard out here, with just Frankie for company most of the day. I miss my friends in Boston, and having you to talk with."

"I wish it were otherwise. My pay isn't as much as

I had hoped. But wives of the other men at the mill seem to make do."

Jake turned and walked toward the back of their property. He didn't want to hear Mother and Father talking about how hard times were. He already knew.

Soon they would have eaten all the squash, and even the pumpkins. Father brought them food each week, but hardly enough for now; certainly not enough to put aside for winter. Massachusetts winters had been long and cold, and Maine was farther north. October was not far away. There wasn't much time to prepare.

Jake wandered into their small orchard. The apples were almost ripe. He'd have to find out how to store them for the winter. The pumpkins, too, if they didn't eat them all first.

He picked a low-hanging apple and bit in. Immediately he spit it out; it was sour and grainy.

He heard giggling.

Turning around, he glimpsed a small figure slipping behind one of the apple trees on the far side of the orchard.

"Violet?" he called.

More giggles. She dodged behind another tree as Jake ran toward her.

She ran around the tree several times as he pretended to try to catch her. When he did, she held one hand behind her back. He spoke sternly. "Violet! Did you take one of my apples?"

"I didn't steal it. I found it on the ground."

"Here, have another one." Jake reached high above his head, picked the reddest apple he could see, and handed it to her.

"Could I have one for Zeke, too? And Nabby? And Ma? We all like apples."

"Violet, don't be greedy. We don't want to take their whole orchard," scolded Nabby, from where the orchard met the meadow. "Thank Jake and come over here."

"It's all right. Really," said Jake, picking several more apples and following Violet. "The apples are still ripening; I just bit into a sour one. I hope these are good. I don't know what to do with so many apples anyway."

Nabby held out her apron as he piled the apples in. "Roasted apples. Cider. Apple dumplings. Apple butter. Dried apples. Applesauce. Apple jelly."

"Do you know how to do all that?" asked Jake.

"Of course. Everyone does." Nabby smiled.

"In Boston we bought such things. Could you teach me? I'll share the apples with you."

"Doesn't your mother know how to cook?"

Jake hesitated. "She's learning."

Nabby didn't seem surprised. "My ma isn't much help either. I'll tell you what to do with the apples."

Her ma wasn't much help? If she'd lived here for some years, wouldn't she know how to cook? Jake let it pass. No doubt Nabby thought it strange his mother was just learning to cook now.

"I'm worried about provisions for the winter," Jake confided.

"What do you need?" Nabby asked.

"Almost everything, starting with food for ourselves and our chickens. Father brings us some food when he comes home each week, but that only helps for the moment."

"Our father brings things home too," said Violet. "Sometimes." She took another bite of the apple.

Nabby looked at her, shook her head slightly, and turned back to Jake. "In winter your father may not be able to come home every week. After mid-November, roads are often deep in snow. Last winter the snow was higher than the first floor of the house. Some used second-floor windows as doors. We dug stairs through the snow so we could climb up onto the frozen drifts, didn't we, Violet?"

Violet nodded, her mouth full of apple.

"Do you know how to find or preserve *anything*?" Nabby asked.

Jake had never thought that Father might not be able to come every Saturday, bringing some of what they needed. Without Father's help he and Mother and Frankie would be in even worse shape than he'd thought. But his pride wouldn't let Nabby know how little they had.

"I can gather oysters," Jake said.

"That's a beginning, and not one many folks here think of. Gather as many fresh oysters as you can, layer them with rockweed and cornmeal, and put them in your cold cellar. If you wet the pile twice a week, they'll last."

"For how long?" asked Jake. Mother and Father wouldn't mind having to eat oysters.

"They'll last through most of the cold weather if you keep them wet," Nabby declared. "They'll freeze, of course, but they'll still be good. You just can't let them dry out. And there are other things from the sea you can put aside for winter too. Mussels. Periwinkles."

"Did your mother teach you all that?"

"No. Granny McPherson did. When times are hard, she knows what to do."

"I'd like to meet her."

"Most boys are scared of Granny," Nabby said seriously.

Violet finished her apple, core and all, and threw the stem on the ground. "Granny McPherson's a witch," she said. "Everyone knows that."

"A witch?" Was Violet serious? He didn't want anything to do with a witch.

"That's what people say," said Nabby. "But she's kind, and she knows more than most folks about getting along."

"Does she live nearby?"

"Beyond your place, a ways off the Alna Road."

A black squirrel dropped from an apple tree and ran just in front of Jake. "What was that?" he said, jumping back. "A cat?"

"Haven't you ever seen a black squirrel?" asked Nabby.

"I've seen gray squirrels and red squirrels. I didn't know there were black squirrels."

"Only a few are born each year. They're slower than their gray cousins. Other squirrels ignore them, or fight with them, so they live alone. But they're squirrels just the same."

"Are they bad luck, like black cats? That squirrel ran right in front of us!" He didn't need any more bad luck.

"Good luck, I think. Rare things are good luck, aren't they?" said Nabby. "Like precious stones."

"That makes sense," Jake agreed, looking after the black squirrel.

"If you'll share your apples, I'll show you what to do with them. But you must share our meat, then," said Nabby. "I don't take charity."

"I didn't mean the apples to be charity," Jake said. "I meant to trade them for advice." But—meat! "Don't you need all the meat you have?"

"I can spare some," Nabby said, and smiled. "If my traps keep working this winter, we'll have rabbit, coon, and sometimes squirrel."

"Will you introduce me to Granny McPherson?"

"She doesn't take to people easily." Nabby hesitated a moment. "But you need help. I think she'll like you."

"When?" asked Jake. Talking with Nabby had made him even more conscious of all that must be done before winter, and he was anxious to meet someone who might be able to help him. "I could come to your house tomorrow."

"I can't always get away," said Nabby quickly. "I'll leave a piece of white cloth tied to this apple tree when we can go the next day. Do you know where the large oak tree is, close to the road, just north of your land?"

"Yes," said Jake. He'd seen the red oak leaves the night he'd raced with Tom.

"I'll meet you there. An hour past supper, the day after you see the white cloth."

❧ 14 ❧

Jake checked the apple tree every day, but Father had come and gone once more before a piece of white cloth was tied to a branch.

All the next day he was anxious. Was Granny McPherson really a witch? Would she really be able to help him? He'd spent the week chopping wood and harvesting oysters. That was a start, but it was clearly not enough to sustain three or four people for months of winter.

He waited by the oak tree for some time before he saw Nabby approaching. She was alone.

"Where are Violet and Zeke?"

"They don't often go to see Granny. They're a little scared of her. Simon is with them, and I promised not to be long."

"Is Simon another brother?" asked Jake.

Nabby shook her head. "Simon's a friend who helps me sometimes."

"Does he live close by?"

"In winter he stays in the tavern stable in town; in summer he sleeps in fields on farms where he can get work. I leave quilts for him in our shed, in case he is nearby and needs shelter. In return he helps me when I need it."

"I'll look forward to meeting him. So far I only know you, and Violet and Zeke, of course, Mrs. Neal, and Tom. And a friend of Tom's—Ed. He said his father was the schoolmaster."

"Ed Holbrook. His father's the Lincoln County jailer as well as the schoolmaster for this district. There are eight districts in Wiscasset. Some of the other schools are larger and have more than one school-master, but they're too far for us to walk to in winter. The Holbrooks live in the house attached to the jail."

"Ed seemed friendly," said Jake.

"Ed's all right when he's alone. But he wants to be like Tom and his friends, and they get him in trouble."

Jake wasn't surprised Tom got people in trouble. "Do you go to the district school?" he asked Nabby.

"When I can," she said. "I try to get the little ones there too, but in the winter snows it can be hard."

"Ed said I'd need supplies for school."

"You'll need a primer and a slate and quills . . . but you probably had all of those in Boston. Mr. Holbrook can tell you what books you'll need," said Nabby. "Lessons won't begin until the end of November. Now's the time to prepare for winter."

She turned where three tall elms stood out from the pine and spruce trees that lined most of the road. A narrow path wound between the trees and back into the pine woods.

"Is this the only way to Granny McPherson's?" asked Jake. "There's no room for a wagon on this path. How does she get supplies? Or visitors?"

"Granny lives her own way," said Nabby. "She doesn't need supplies she can't find on her own, and she has few guests." She shrugged. "It isn't easy to be different from other people."

Jake looked at her. "No."

"When Granny goes to town, there are some who call her names. Sometimes they throw stones at her."

"That's awful!"

"Yes. If she were truly a witch she'd do something to stop it."

"Like turning those people into hogs?"

Nabby laughed. "Some of those boys would fit right into a hog family!"

The path widened a little before reaching a small log house, almost hidden under the trees. Its roof was covered with pine needles, and its sides were banked with spruce boughs so thick you had to look carefully to see the door and two small windows.

Nabby rapped on the door. "Granny! Granny, it's Nabby! I've brought someone to meet you!"

The door opened slowly. "Someone to meet me?"

The door opened a little wider. "He isn't one of those nasty boys from down at the school, is he?"

"No," said Nabby. "I wouldn't bring one of those boys here. Jake just moved to Wiscasset from Boston. He needs your help."

The door finally opened wide. Jake tried to be brave. He understood why some people thought Granny McPherson strange. She didn't look like any woman he'd ever met.

She was short, and thin, and old. Her back was bent, her face brown and wrinkled, and her long gray hair fell down her back in two thin braids. She wore a heavy woven shawl and a long skirt. Both were black. She did look like a witch.

"Come on in then, girl, and bring your friend." She looked Jake up and down, as he was looking at her. "What do you want with an old woman who lives in the woods?"

"Nabby said you'd helped her find food for her family. I need to do that too."

"It's the beginning of October, boy. Frost is in the ground, and crickets are singing their good-byes. Not much you can do now."

"But I have to have food for the winter!" blurted Jake. "My family is hungry!" If this strange woman couldn't help, then who would?

"The earth always provides something. Deer eat the bark off trees," said Granny McPherson.

"Bark!"

Granny's eyes twinkled at Jake's reaction. "Sit. Have some of my special cider."

"Take just a little cider," whispered Nabby as she pushed Jake ahead of her. "It's strong, and she doesn't water it for children."

The house was one room, low and dark and hung with dried plants.

Jake nodded slightly. "Just a small amount, please," he said. "Nabby, aren't you going to have any?"

"I don't drink cider," said Nabby. "Could I have a mug of water, Granny?"

"You never change, girl," said Granny, approvingly. "How is your mother? And those two youngsters?"

"Everyone is fine. I brought Jake so you could advise him what he could do so late in the season."

"Do you live alone, boy?" she said, handing Jake a clay mug holding a pale yellow liquid. "Where are your ma and pa, who should be worrying about such things as food for the winter?"

Jake sniffed the cider, and then took a sip. Nabby was right. Granny's cider was strong but good.

Granny sat next to him and leaned her walking stick on the table. It was covered with carvings of human and animal faces. A dark cat moved from a corner and jumped onto her lap. Jake started. He hadn't seen the cat before it jumped. But it was just a cat. A black cat.

He put his mug down on the hand-hewn table.

What if Granny *were* a witch? Why wasn't Nabby drinking even a little of the cider? What if his mug was poisoned? What if Nabby had lured him to this place? They were so far in the woods no one would find him.

"Can't you talk, boy?"

Jake reached for the mug and swallowed a little more of the cider. He wasn't afraid of any old woman. "My father lost his job in Boston. President Van Buren says better times are coming, but they haven't yet. Father's cousin, Ben Webber, got him a job at a mill here in Wiscasset, and we moved here last month."

"Jake lives close by me," added Nabby.

"Father's at the mill all week, and Mother has to stay home, and she never had to do much cooking before now. They're from the city, and they don't know country ways. They don't know what we need to get by."

Granny didn't ask why Mother had to stay home, or why they couldn't ask someone else for help. "So you have little money and no skills. And your pa's away most of the week."

"But I've already learned to chop wood, and Mother can make a fire, and she's getting better at cooking. She bakes bread almost every day. We got four chickens, and I made them a house. And I know how to find oysters."

"So you're eating eggs and bread and oysters." Granny took a noisy sip of the cider in her own mug.

"And squash from the garden, but we've almost finished those."

"They have a small apple orchard," put in Nabby. "I'll teach him to dry apples and store some for steaming and baking and sauce."

"That'll be a start. And you told him how to keep oysters in seaweed?"

"I did."

"Not many here know that," Granny added. "I taught Nabby." She looked at Jake. "Can you shoot? Arrows or bullets?"

"No," said Jake.

"Deer and bear are good meat, for those willing to hunt and clean the animals," said Granny. "Most folks near here are too modern to be interested in hunting. Leaves more for the rest of us."

"I can show him how to trap," said Nabby. "Squirrel is good eating on a cold day."

"True enough. And this is the time of year chucks and squirrels and rabbits are fat and slow. They're readying for the winter too."

Jake nodded slowly.

"This year you'll have to trap. But remember, it's fairer to the animals if you give 'em a chance by hunting 'em. They'll understand. Just take no more than you and your family can eat. One of your neighbors should have damaged ears of corn you can use to bait your traps."

Eating rabbits and woodchucks and squirrels! His Boston friends wouldn't believe how he was living now. But if Nabby could do it, then he must too.

Granny McPherson looked at Jake. "You'll have to skin and clean those animals, and then salt them. If you have no salt, wash the flesh in salt water and hang it in your chimney to smoke. And you can do with mussels the same as you do with oysters. You'll need more mussels to fill you than you would of oysters, but they can be roasted or stewed just the same. Make sure you only harvest the blue mussels, not the brown."

Jake had never heard of anyone eating mussels. He didn't even know there were both brown and blue.

"You'll find other foods on the shore," Granny continued. "Rockweed brews up to a nice tea. Dry it or boil it fresh. And Irish moss; Nabby will show you what Irish moss looks like."

Nabby nodded. "I will."

"It's a sea plant that's curly and tough and tastes something awful if you don't cook it long, but it's strengthening. Harvest it now, wash it good in fresh water, and then leave it to dry. In the winter chop it and boil it up, and it'll make a pudding. Or add a little to water to make a tea. It'll thicken a soup up nice too. Can you get any fish?"

"I don't have a boat."

"Next year, you find someone with a boat who'll take you out. Then you can dry or salt fish, too."

Granny hesitated, thinking of what else could still be done this late in the fall. "There may still be rose hips. You gathered yours yet, girl?"

"Some."

"Your mother should be drinking rose hip tea every day. Go together, then, and collect what you can. You can tell Jake how to boil the hips to make syrup for tea."

"They make a nice sauce for bread too," added Nabby. "I gathered some in August, but there are more on rosebushes down by the old Linden place, I think."

"How do you know all these things, Granny?" asked Jake.

"My people always lived in these woods, and survived as best they could. It's living with people in towns that's hard."

Jake took another sip of cider.

Granny startled him with her next question. "Does your father bring home money from that mill he works in, or does he drink it?"

"He's not a drinking man! He brings home food. Salt pork, sometimes, and wheat flour, and sugar. Tea, when he can."

"Tell him to take what money he has and buy dried peas and beans, and cornmeal. They'll keep your insides warm and full for the winter. Sugar and tea you don't need." Granny shook her head. "Molasses will do as well as sugar for sweetening, and it's not so dear."

What would Mother say to that? Her tea with sugar

was a precious reminder of what their life had been. Mother could give up beef, he suspected, but not her tea and sugar.

"You said your ma bakes bread?"

"She's getting better at it every time," said Jake proudly.

"Tell her to make corn bread. Cornmeal makes bread that's tastier and sticks to you more than wheat. Do you have rough corn and oats for your chickens?"

"I have ground oyster shells," Jake said. "For now the chickens eat grasses."

"Soon grasses will be brown and covered with snow and ice. And you'll have no eggs if there's no grain. Buy or trade for oats for the chickens. Any extra oats can be for bread or porridge."

"I'll remember." Jake took another sip of cider. "There's so much to do."

"When you have to eat and you have responsibility for others, then you find a way to manage," said Granny, rising. "You know where I am now, Jake, but I don't expect to see you soon. This season is one for preparing for quieter times. If the weather agrees, you stop by with Nabby in winter."

"Thank you for helping," said Jake.

"You'll winter well," said Granny. "You're strong. You'll endure, and spring will come. By then you should know more, and be better prepared."

"Prepared to find different kinds of food?"

"Prepared for life."

❖ 15 ❖

"Does Granny McPherson ever go to Wiscasset?" asked Jake as he and Nabby headed home.

"Seldom," said Nabby. "But people in the village seek her out when they need herbs for medicine. She and Dr. Theobold treat sicknesses in different ways, and sometimes her potions and salves work when his ways don't."

Did she have anything that would help Frankie's fits? Jake determined to go back and talk with her privately, after he had more food put away. Surely Mother wouldn't mind his talking to a healer.

"How old is she?"

"As old as her memories. No one knows."

"McPherson sounds like an Irish name," Jake mused.

"Scots, she once told me. Her husband was a hunter and trapper from Scotland." Nabby looked at Jake sidewise. "She's Penobscot, you know."

"She's what?"

"Penobscot. Indians who used to live north of here."

"Oh." Jake didn't think he'd ever met an Indian before. But maybe that explained why Granny McPherson lived in such an isolated place. "Aren't any of her people left?"

"Few near here."

Jake nodded.

"She told me her people were like barnacles, clinging to the land and rocks of Maine as the winds gusted and seas crashed over them. Sometimes it seemed impossible that they'd survive. But barnacles are strong, and take their food from the waters, so without tides they would die."

Jake liked that thought. Some days he felt like one of those barnacles being hit by the spray and surf.

"I'll teach you about trapping," said Nabby, "but tomorrow I have chores to do. I mustn't be away from home two days in a row, and Simon can't be counted on to help. He needs to work where he is paid. Watch for the white tie on the tree. After you see it, we'll meet."

"You've helped a lot already. You and Granny. I'll watch for your signal." He paused. "But even if I do all the things you and Granny have told me about, we'll still need grain and seasonings and candles and whale oil. Father has to pay for board and room near the mill, and there isn't enough left to buy everything we need."

"That's often the case with menfolk who work outside town," said Nabby. "Women work out of their homes, so they can keep more of what they earn."

"Do you or your mother work at home? I mean, for money?"

"Mother used to weave coverlets," Nabby said. "But no more. And my time is filled gathering food and cooking and caring for Violet and Zeke. I'm knitting stockings now that the children will need before the snows. But that's for the family, not for sale."

Nabby spoke of "the children" as a mother or father might. "How old are you?" Jake asked.

She shook her head. "Granny would say age is just a measure of time. It doesn't tell who you are or what you can do." She looked at him and smiled. "I'm eleven. And you?"

"Almost thirteen," said Jake.

When they came to the wagon path to Jake's house, they separated, each returning to their own families and concerns.

❖ 16 ❖

Jake pulled his jacket around him. What had been sea breezes in early September became dank winds in October. He quickened his steps and wondered how cold winter gales would be.

He'd just started down the road when he saw Mrs. Neal, walking far ahead of him but toward his home.

Jake turned and ran home, slamming the door closed behind him.

"What is happening, Jake? Are you all right?" Mother was sitting on the floor, holding Frankie. She'd just fed him some water-soaked bread for breakfast. "I thought you were going to visit Nabby."

Jake had planned another destination for the day, but was afraid Mother wouldn't approve, so he'd told her he hadn't seen Nabby recently. In truth there had been no white cloth on the apple tree for the past week.

"I just saw Mrs. Neal in the road," Jake gasped. "She was walking this way. I think she's coming to visit you."

Mother handed Frankie to Jake and stood up. "Quickly, put Frankie on a quilt on the floor next to the bedstead," she said. "Cover his legs with blankets so he won't be cold."

Jake carried Frankie into the bedroom. Father was the only one who slept there, and the room was chilly and damp. Jake pulled blankets and quilts off the bed and tucked them around Frankie.

Mother pulled clouts off the rope she had left up in one corner of their main room to dry clothes. No one would have clouts drying unless they had a baby. Or unless they had Frankie. "Is Frankie all right?"

"He moved a little, but he's quiet," said Jake.

"Luckily he's just eaten," said Mother. "Here, help me move the screen so it covers most of the pallets in his corner."

The screen covered some of the pallets, but not all of them.

Mother's hands shook as she pulled up her hair and straightened her apron. "Go and pump some fresh water for the kettle. We must offer Mrs. Neal some tea," she said.

Jake was pumping the water when Mrs. Neal appeared around the bend in the drive, carrying a basket.

"Jake! How nice to see you. I've come to call on your mother."

"Of course. It's good to see you, Mrs. Neal," said Jake, holding the kettle and reaching to open the door for her. "Mother, we have company! This is Mrs. Neal, our neighbor who was so kind to us when we first arrived."

Mother had composed herself and managed to get out her best teapot. She welcomed Mrs. Neal as though they were in a Boston sitting room.

"How lovely of you to have stopped in, Mrs. Neal," Mother said. "I was just about to have a cup of tea. I hope you'll join me?"

"I would love to." Mrs. Neal looked around the room but made no comment about the rope line that was still hanging there, or the strange pile of pallets in one corner. "I've brought you some blackberry jam, and some fiddlehead pickles I made last spring."

"Oh, how lovely," Mother said. "Thank you! Perhaps we can have some of the jam on a slice of the bread I made this morning."

She went to the sideboard and got out the mahogany caddy she still used for tea, a tea strainer, two silver spoons, and a small knife for spreading. Jake hadn't seen their silver spoons or knives since they'd arrived in Maine. They had been using pewter ones.

Jake hung the kettle on the crane in the fireplace.

"Won't you sit down?" Mother gestured to Mrs. Neal. "I'm afraid we don't have a lot of space here, but there are just the three of us, after all."

Jake winced slightly. Mother had not included Frankie in the family.

There was a slight groan from Frankie in the other

room. Mother ignored the sound, but Mrs. Neal looked up. She had heard something.

"Old houses make the strangest sounds, don't they?" Mother asked. She talked quickly to distract Mrs. Neal, and to cover any other noises Frankie might make. "Jake, there's some straightening up to do in the other room. Perhaps you could take care of it while Mrs. Neal and I get to know each other?"

Jake nodded. He understood: He was to make sure Frankie kept quiet. "It was nice to see you again, Mrs. Neal," he said as he left the room, making sure to open and shut the door quietly.

Jake took another blanket from the large bed, folded it, and covered Frankie in one more layer. Frankie was sleeping, so maybe all would be well. But how could he stop Frankie from making noises in his sleep?

He tried to listen to Mother and Mrs. Neal talking in the other room, but with the door closed he couldn't hear much.

Frankie murmured, and moved slightly in his sleep. Jake prayed he wouldn't have one of his fits. Then he realized the best way to keep Mrs. Neal from hearing Frankie was to make other noises. At first he paced up and down the room loudly. But the sound of his boots on the floor was too loud, and it might wake Frankie. What did Mother do to quiet him?

Jake started singing softly. At first he sang Mother Goose rhymes, but then he realized Mrs. Neal would think that odd. Why would a boy of twelve be singing nursery rhymes? He switched to hymns. Better Mrs. Neal thought he was very religious than think he was childish. He sang louder every time Frankie moved or moaned.

He had sung every song he could think of, including three stanzas of "Blest Be the Tie That Binds," when Mother opened the door.

"She's left," Mother said. "You did well. Although I do think Mrs. Neal thought it odd that you were singing so loud in the next room!" She picked up Frankie and carried him back to his place in the front room. "And you did well too, my poor dear." Jake moved the screen so she could put the boy back on his pallet. "Mrs. Neal seems pleasant enough. I was nervous, so I wasn't as gracious a hostess as I might have been. I'm sure she left thinking I'd rushed her out, and that we were a bit odd, what with my drinking tea twice as fast as usual, and your singing."

Jake grinned. "But we did it."

"We did," agreed Mother. "Now let's just hope Mrs. Neal isn't kind enough to pay us another call soon!"

❧ 17 ❧

Jake stayed home long enough to devour two slices of bread with blackberry jam. He hadn't eaten anything sweet since Mrs. Neal had given them a pie. He could have eaten two more slices, but he knew Mother was also craving sweetness. She added a bit of extra sugar to a second cup of tea.

"Thank goodness you spotted Mrs. Neal as you started to leave," Mother said, relief filling her voice. "What if Mrs. Neal had just knocked on the door?"

Neither of them said anything, thinking of that possibility.

"You could have pretended not to be here. Maybe you were in the orchard. After all, the curtains on the windows do keep someone from looking in."

"I'm just afraid that she would have walked in anyway," said Mother. "I remember from Framingham that country people don't even seem to be embarrassed about such details as whether someone is in the privy or not."

It was chance that he'd seen Mrs. Neal. A lucky chance.

"You go ahead and visit Nabby now," Mother said. "I'll hang the clouts up again and straighten the bed clothing we borrowed for Frankie from the other room."

Jake nodded and started out again. He looked for Nabby as he passed her house, but all was quiet, and then he sprinted by the Neals' house. He didn't want to see Mrs. Neal again, and he didn't want to run into Tom.

After another mile he saw what he was looking for. Near the road, on a slope overlooking the Sheepscot River, was the Lincoln County Jail and the jailer's house. The jail was a forbidding place, dark and high.

The two bottom stories of the jail were made of large granite blocks. The third and fourth floors were wood, as was the roof. Jake looked at the narrow barred windows and questioned whether his plan was a wise one.

The two-story wooden jailer's house was connected to the prison so the jailer could check on the prisoners and attend to their needs without having to go outside, and the kitchen that served the jailer and his wife and children also served the inmates.

A three-sided fence was on the far end of the jail; its fourth side was the back of the building. Solid timbers ten or eleven feet high were topped with a plank covered by long spikes whose sharp ends rose another eight inches.

One entrance served for both buildings. Jake raised the heavy iron door-knocker and let it fall.

The man who answered was taller than Father and had a deep voice and wide shoulders. "What can I do for you?"

"I'm looking for Mr. Holbrook."

"You've found him." Mr. Holbrook opened the door and gestured for Jake to enter. "I don't know you, and I know most of the boys who live hereabouts. Would you be the one my son, Ed, said moved into the old Crocker place?"

"I would," answered Jake. "My name's Jake Webber." Had Ed told his father of Jake's getting stuck in the mudflats? "My parents and I moved here from Boston in early September."

"Then, welcome to Wiscasset," said Mr. Holbrook. "Are you making a social call, or have you business at the jail?" He smiled as though he were jesting, and waved Jake into a sitting room to his right. On his left was a larger heavy iron door with forged iron hinges and latches and two locks. *That must be the entrance to the prison,* Jake thought.

Jake smelled stew, and heard small feet running on the floor above him.

"I came on business," Jake said firmly.

"Then, please sit," said Mr. Holbrook, settling into

a straight pine chair next to a round table piled with red and blue leather-bound books, a pile of papers, an inkwell, and two quill pens. He gestured that Jake should sit on a long bench near the stove. Jake was glad of the warmth. He put his hands out toward the stove and rubbed them together for a moment before turning back to Mr. Holbrook.

"I've heard you're the schoolmaster for this district of Wiscasset, as well as the county jailer."

"I've been a schoolmaster longer than a jailer, but Wiscasset was in need of both, so I agreed to take on two jobs. I hope you'll be attending our school. The winter session starts six weeks from now."

"Nabby McCord tells me supplies are required."

Holbrook looked at Jake. "The usual: ink, slates, and primers for mathematics and reading, depending on your abilities. Mrs. Ames has a flock of geese and sends me enough quills for everyone. Have you attended school before?"

"I studied at an academy in Boston." Jake hesitated. "I can read well, and calculate. I've been studying geography and history, and I can read some Latin, but no Greek."

Mr. Holbrook shook his head. "I only run a district school aimed at teaching basic reading and ciphering. There are academies and tutors in Wiscasset that would be more suited to your needs."

"I'm going to be forthright, Mr. Holbrook." The

sound of giggling and stomping above made Jake look up.

"My children are playing games. You've met Edwin, my oldest. Annie is five, and Margaret two. Mrs. Holbrook and I hope to be blessed with another child early in 1839." Mr. Holbrook was clearly proud of his children. "Are there other Webbers I can look forward to meeting?"

"I'll be the only one attending school," Jake said quickly. "And I would like to join your classes. My family has suffered financial reversals in the past year; academies and tutors are not possible for us just now."

Mr. Holbrook nodded. "The country is going through difficult times. President Van Buren is trying to create a national treasury system separate from the banks. I believe his ideas will work, but they're far from being accepted. The crisis will not end soon."

"My father worked for one of the banks that failed."

"I'm sorry. I've heard many have lost jobs, particularly in the cities."

"We came here because there was work for Father at the mill. But we have no money for new books."

Mr. Holbrook paused. "There are other students in the district with limited funds, and often they share books, or borrow those of students who have completed the lessons. But your skills are too advanced for such measures. I do have some books of history you could borrow, and I would enjoy having a Latin scholar to work with, perhaps after regular class hours. It would help me review my own skills."

"That would be very generous of you." Jake paused. "I have a copy of Nathaniel Hawthorne's *Twice-Told Tales* I could share." Jake hesitated again. "It's my favorite book."

"Excellent. I don't think any of my scholars are ready to read Mr. Hawthorne on their own, but they would enjoy hearing his stories. He may live in Massachusetts, but he's a Mainer at heart, you know. Spent a year or two in Maine when he wasn't much older than you, and is a graduate of Bowdoin College. Perhaps you could read some of his less frightening stories to the class."

"Thank you, Mr. Holbrook! I would be happy to read to the younger students. And I would appreciate any extra help you could give me." Jake relaxed somewhat. Mr. Holbrook was being very understanding about his plight. "I do have a Latin dictionary. Before the Panic I was preparing for college. Maybe Harvard, or Bowdoin."

"I will help as best I can, Jake." Mr. Holbrook started to get up.

"But . . . no." Jake stopped him. "School is not all I came to discuss. I must get enough money to buy corn for traps, and salt to preserve whatever meat I can bring home. Our chickens need oats, and we should have stores of cornmeal and dried peas and beans for the winter. . . ."

Mr. Holbrook looked at him. "You're new to country living."

"But I'm a hard worker, and I've found out what I must do. I came to ask if you knew of anyone looking for help. I need money."

"Is all well with your parents?"

"Father brings home some dollars and essentials each week. And Nabby McCord is helping me learn how to collect and preserve food. But my family still has needs that we can't meet."

Mr. Holbrook paused and listened to the commotion above for a moment. There was a ball bouncing upstairs. He looked back at Jake. "Nabby's a special young woman."

"She is," agreed Jake.

"Did she suggest you talk with me?"

"No. That was my idea, after Ed told me you were both the jailer and the schoolmaster. I came to talk with you about school. And also"—Jake paused—"to ask if you knew anywhere I could work. I'm almost thirteen, I'm strong, and I'm willing to do anything needed."

Mr. Holbrook got up and paced a bit.

Jake sat quietly, rubbing his hands together with nervousness and cold.

"Clearly you have responsibilities at home," said **Mr. Holbrook.**

"I can meet needs there early and late in the day. We need money to purchase additional provisions."

What would Father or Mother think if they knew Jake was admitting their financial situation to someone outside the family? But he had made his choice. He hoped it was the right one. He was doing what was necessary.

"Your family must be proud of what you're doing for them." Mr. Holbrook shook his head slightly. "And Nabby, too. Those who feel childhood is only a time for games do not know its realities." The happy giggling of his daughters, and a hoot of laughter from Ed, filled the silence. "I could find work for you here at the jail, but it is not pleasant work. It would mean cleaning cells and emptying chamber pots and answering the needs of those who are criminals, and those who are insane."

Could he do that? Jake remembered feeling uncomfortable seeing the homeless and confused in the streets of Boston. Here he would be working with those who were not only confused but possibly violent.

But Mother and Frankie were at home. Waiting for him to provide.

"I can clean cells," said Jake. "I can do whatever has to be done."

"You'll still need time at home, to care for your family," said Mr. Holbrook. "But if you could come here every other day, it would help both of us. I could use the extra time to prepare for my classes."

"I understand."

"Good. You may begin Monday morning."

Jake stood and reached out his hand. "Thank you, sir. I won't let you down."

"I don't believe you will, Jake. That's why I'm hiring you."

❧ 18 ❧

"But, Jake, will you be safe?" Mother frowned after he'd told her about his job at the prison.

"We need the money. And I'll only spend three or four days a week there. The other days I can work here. Nabby's going to teach me how to trap, so we can have meat."

Mother paled visibly. "Trap what?"

"Squirrels, she said. Woodchucks. Rabbits. Maybe raccoons."

"We're going to eat squirrels and woodchucks? Jake—I can't. Only wild Indians eat animals like that!"

Jake decided not to mention Granny McPherson.

"Who will skin them? And clean them? And cook them?"

"Nabby will show me how to skin and clean them," said Jake. "And you can cook them, Mother. It'll be like boiling or roasting chicken. If I get enough meat, we'll smoke some by hanging it in the chimney. That will keep it from spoiling."

Mother shook her head. "Eating squirrel! I never thought I'd be reduced to eating squirrel! Remember the parties we used to have, Jake? All the candles and music and elegant dresses?"

"And we have lots of apples," Jake went on. "Some we can peel and slice and hang in the loft to dry."

Mother brightened at that. "I can peel and slice apples," she agreed. "And they'll be good all winter. We can put some whole apples in the cellar, too; the ground is already cold, and they'll store well down there."

"So I hope," agreed Jake. "I'll cut some dried grasses to layer with them so air can circulate. We can store the pumpkins we have left too."

"And you can keep oysters?"

"And mussels, I've heard," said Jake. "I'll take our wagon down to the shore and collect what I can." He remembered what Granny had said. "There are seaweeds that make good teas. I'll try to find some of those. We can dry them for the winter."

Mother wrinkled her nose again. "Seaweed tea?"

"It won't be like the tea you're accustomed to," admitted Jake, "but it will cost less and be a warm drink in winter. Seaweed tea is strengthening." He noticed Mother's quizzical look. "Some say."

"Who are these people you've been talking to?" she asked. "They have some strange ideas of what can be eaten, and what is healthy."

"Nabby and a friend of hers," said Jake. "Nabby knows where there are rose hips, for another tea."

"Rose hip tea?" Mother smiled. "*That* I've heard of. A friend of my mother's was quite fond of it. She drank it with honey."

"Maybe I'll be able to get some honey when I get paid," said Jake. "But first we need to get corn for the traps. And I've been thinking we could get a few more chickens. We have space, and we have the ground oyster shells now. Then we'd have more eggs, and the chickens could be meat if we had nothing else left."

"No more chickens until we see how the rest of your plans work," advised Mother. "All these projects will take time, and you're now committed to being away from home half the week."

"And I must find dry wood and chop it to size for the fireplace," Jake continued, getting excited about all the possibilities. "The woodpile I've made so far will hardly get us through a month or two."

Mother brightened. "I know how to knit! My aunt taught me, when I was small. Somewhere I have the needles my uncle carved for me. If I had some wool, I could knit socks for all of us."

"I'll ask Nabby who spins the yarn she uses."

Mother looked pleased that she'd thought of knitting. "Your brother has been well these past days. He hasn't had any fits, and he's been able to swallow egg and a little bread with water."

Frankie was lying on the floor, his eyes wide open. They had never been sure Frankie could see anything more than light, which he turned toward. But he could hear their voices, and he moved his head when he heard his name. What would life have been like for all of them if Frankie were like other six-year-old boys?

He would have been able to play marbles, and bring in water, and help find oysters and pick apples. He'd be planning to go to school with Jake in six weeks. Jake could have taught him to read and cipher.

And Mother wouldn't be so tired and pale, and unable to leave the house for more than a few moments.

But even if Frankie would never be like other boys, maybe there was some way to make his life, and that of his family, easier. Maybe Granny McPherson had a remedy.

Surely Frankie needed more help than anyone.

❧ 19 ❧

Saturday morning Jake added branches and logs to their woodpile while Mother baked bread and stewed apples with the little sugar they had left. Then she straightened the house as best she could, put on a good dress, and sat, waiting for Father.

He arrived late Saturday afternoon, weary as always, carrying bundles of food and candles. This Saturday he had a letter for Mother that had been left at the post office in town.

Jake pumped water for Father to use to wash up as Mother sat quietly, reading the letter over and over.

"What does your sister in Framingham have to say?" asked Father, drying his face and neck.

"Elizabeth and the rest of the family are well," said Mother. "Annie Pease and Aaron Brown are engaged, and little William just got over the measles."

"That's good," said Father, sitting at the table and sipping the cold water Jake had left him.

Mother put the letter on the table. "Nathaniel, I miss seeing everyone. So much."

"Maybe next summer Elizabeth could visit us."

Mother looked around the room. "No, Nathaniel. They know we were hurt by the Panic, but they don't know we're living like this."

"I'm doing better at the mill. I've asked for more responsibilities there, so perhaps soon I'll be earning higher wages."

"Still. Wiscasset will never be Boston."

"No. But Maine is a state with possibilities, and I won't be operating saws at the mill forever," said Father.

"Jake planned to go to college."

"And he still can! Just maybe a few years later than we'd hoped."

Jake had been listening from Frankie's corner, where he was lightly stroking his brother's arm. "I've talked to the schoolmaster for the local district school, Father. He's agreed to help me with history and Latin after regular hours."

"That's good, Jake."

"Mr. Holbrook says there are tutors and an academy in the village where students prepare for college."

Father sighed. "Maybe by next year we can afford a school like that."

Jake took a deep breath, and glanced at Mother for support. How would Father react to the rest of his news? "And that's not the best of it! Mr. Holbrook's given me a job."

"At the school?"

"At the jail. Mr. Holbrook's also the jailer for Lincoln County. I'll work there every other day, beginning Monday."

"At the jail! With prisoners?" Father pushed his chair back and got up from the table. "I can't allow my son to work at a prison!"

"I'll be safe, Father. I will. Mr. Holbrook's wife and children live in the house connected to the jail. You pass it every weekend."

Father sat down again, heavily.

"With the money I earn I can buy some of what we need," said Jake.

"Are you saying I'm not providing for my family?" said Father.

Mother interrupted him. "Jake's almost thirteen, Nathaniel. Many boys his age bring home wages. Perhaps he could put away some money for school. He's been working so hard to help us."

"If I were earning more money, my boy wouldn't have to work when he should be studying."

"I'll be studying, too, Father."

They were all silent for a few minutes.

"I'm going for a walk," said Father.

Mother rose to go with him.

"Alone," Father said.

❈ 20 ❈

Monday morning Jake got up with the rooster, made sure the chickens had fresh water and ground oyster shells and the little corn he'd found in the garden, and picked a wagonload of apples for Mother to peel, core, slice, and string.

It was almost seven when he rapped on the jail door.

A woman who was clearly in the family way opened the door, pulling a blue shawl around her shoulders. The shawl matched her eyes. He'd never paid attention to eyes before, but Mrs. Holbrook—it must be Mrs. Holbrook—had beautiful eyes. What color were his mother's eyes? He wasn't even sure.

"Jake?"

"Yes, ma'am." Jake realized he was staring at her. "I was expecting Mr. Holbrook."

"He's already at the jail, giving the inmates their breakfasts. I'm Mrs. Holbrook."

"Pleased to meet you," said Jake. "I'm here to help."

"So I hear, and we can use you. Mr. Holbrook doesn't allow any of us to enter the jail without him, or even to open the door." She gestured at the large iron door inside the entryway. "While you're waiting for him, I have some chores for you to do," she added.

Jake followed her through the sitting room and dining room, and then into a warm kitchen filled with the smell of rising anadama bread. Jake's mouth watered, although he'd already eaten three slices of bread at home. Perhaps when he or father bought some cornmeal, Mother would make anadama bread too.

"I've been baking this morning, so the wood box needs filling," said Mrs. Holbrook. "You'll find the woodpile beyond the outbuildings. Bring the wood in and fill the box next to the stove until no more will fit. I'll be upstairs with the children. When you finish, pump enough water to fill the large basin next to the stove so I can heat water for washing. When you have a little one there are always clouts to wash." She patted her rising stomach. "Carrying water is difficult for me now."

"Yes, ma'am," said Jake, blushing at her reference to the baby to come, and thinking of the clouts his mother washed at home. Frankie would always need to wear them. Mrs. Holbrook's little girl and her baby-to-come would learn to use chamber pots and privies.

"If Mr. Holbrook hasn't returned by the time you finish, call up the stairs to me."

"Yes, ma'am," said Jake. He wondered why she hadn't asked Ed to fill the wood box. He had thought all his work would be in the jail. Clearly he was to do whatever the Holbrooks needed done.

Their woodpile was twenty times bigger than his. How could his family keep warm this winter?

But his home had only one fireplace. The Holbrooks had a large stove in their kitchen, another in the dining room, and the one he'd warmed his hands at in the living room. There might be more stoves in the rooms above. Plus, Jake realized, there must be stoves on the jail side of the building as well. Even prisoners had to have warmth in the winter, and the Holbrooks' woodpile had to supply both their home and the jail.

After filling the wood box, Jake took a bucket and filled the basin from the pump in the kitchen.

He'd forgotten the ease of not having to go outside to pump water. He'd also forgotten the luxury of having a maid bring a filled pitcher and a basin to his room so he could wash when he woke in the morning. It must have been heavy work for his family's maids in Boston to lug water up two flights from the kitchen, and then to remove the waste, along with the slops in the chamber pot.

How those maids would laugh to see him now. Jake grinned a little to himself. Pride and status seemed unimportant in the face of hunger and cold.

"Jake? Have you finished the jobs my wife needed

done?" Mr. Holbrook entered the kitchen holding a stack of dirty tin bowls.

"Yes, sir. The wood box is full, and the water is ready to be heated."

"Good. I'll introduce you to the jail, and its inmates. That's where most of your work will be."

Mr. Holbrook opened the thick iron door just inside the main entrance to the building.

"The jail is built so I can enter it from the first floor of the house," explained Mr. Holbrook. "I keep the keys with me whenever I'm to home. If I'm away, they're in our kitchen, on a high shelf. No one but me, or Sheriff Beals, should ever open the main door. You will only work in the jail when I am here."

"Yes, sir." Jake had no desire to go into the prison alone.

The air inside the jail was heavy with dampness. Rock walls and floor held moisture far longer than wood. As Mr. Holbrook locked the heavy door from the inside, Jake looked at the stone steps that led up and down. The jail was on a hill, so the lowest floor of cells was lower than the first floor of the house, and almost like a cellar. On the wall along the stairs hung an assortment of leather and iron restraints, and ropes of different lengths.

Mr. Holbrook watched him. "Are you all right with this? No one but you and I, or lawyers, doctors, and close family of the inmates, come here."

"How many prisoners are there?" Jake asked.

"I'll show you."

Jake followed Mr. Holbrook down the stairs. At the bottom of the steps was another thick iron door, barred and locked.

The door creaked as Mr. Holbrook pushed it open for Jake. A cold iron stove stood in the corner of the granite hallway.

"Later in the fall one of your jobs will be to keep the stoves going," said Mr. Holbrook.

Jake wondered how cold temperatures would have to be to justify fires. The floor felt cold to him now.

"Who're you talking at, Holbrook? Someone got a visitor?"

A woman's loud voice came from behind one of the six iron doors that lined the passageway. Jake shook, from either cold or fear. He wasn't sure which.

Mr. Holbrook ignored the voice. "This level of the jail is the coldest in winter, and the dampest, so we keep prisoners here who've committed the most serious offenses."

"There are six cells," said Jake, almost whispering. He felt as though he were in church. His voice echoed against the stone walls.

"Yes. Usually we have one person in each cell, but when there's an emergency, like when a dozen sailors got drunk and started to tear up Whittier's Tavern last month, I put as many in a cell as can fit."

"Who've you got there, I'm asking?" yelled the voice again. "Is that my son, come to get me out of this place?"

"It's not your son, Margaret," called Mr. Holbrook. "It's Jake Webber. He's going to help me keep this place in order."

Margaret's voice got softer, and then rose shrilly. "Is Jake young and handsome, then? If I'm bound to stay here longer, a young handsome face would ease the aggravation of dealing with such as *you*!"

Jake tried to smile. "Who is she?" he whispered.

"Margaret Flanders," said Mr. Holbrook. "Margaret's a regular guest here, right Margaret?"

"Three meals a day, and if you're nice, Holbrook brings a blanket or two," agreed Margaret's voice from the second cell on the right. "But I'm tired of his hospitality. I want to go *home*!"

"In another week, Margaret," said Holbrook. To Jake, he added, "Margaret likes fires. We have the pleasure of her company several times a year, after she burns someone's barn down. She's from Waldoboro."

He opened the cell next to Margaret's, which was unlocked. It was empty, a cold dark granite box. The only light was from a small barred window high on the outside wall, just above ground level.

"You will scrub the cells, empty the slop pails, and wash down the bedsteads to keep bugs to a minimum. The inmates won't be in their cells while you're cleaning them. I'll either move them to the outside yard or, in bad weather, to an empty cell."

"I can scrub cells." At least he wouldn't have direct contact with the prisoners.

Holbrook hesitated. "The cleaning will not be pleasant. In some cells you'll find food and slops on the floor or the bed. We change the pallets in spring, but they have to last until then. And if an inmate is ill, or angry . . ." He shook his head. "Just do the best you can. And keep your eyes open for anything that shouldn't be in a cell—a weapon, or even a sharp spoon. If you're in doubt about anything, remove it and show it to me."

Jake nodded.

"You'll also deliver meals to the inmates. They can be pushed through the small wooden doors at the bottom of the cell doors."

Jake noted the small sliding doors that were just narrow enough for a tin dish. "The prisoners are supposed to push their dishes back into the hall when they're finished, but often they do not. Those you'll find when you clean the cells."

"I can do that," said Jake softly. The tasks did not sound pleasant, but they didn't sound impossible, either.

"So you're telling the boy all he has to do, Holbrook," came another voice, this one young but rasping. "Are you also warning him about the evils we inmates can be telling him? Quite an education we could give a young man!" said the voice, chuckling deeply before the chuckle turned into a cough.

Jake looked at Mr. Holbrook, questioningly.

"Thomas Wilson's a thief. Only eighteen but old in prison experience. It's his third trip here." He walked over to the cell beyond Margaret's. "Thomas, that cough sounds worse. Are you in need of the doctor?"

"Not much he can do for me," said Thomas. "A warm drink would help somewhat."

"I'll try to make the time to get you one," said Holbrook.

He unlocked the door and led Jake back to the stairway. "Thomas has been coughing for three weeks now. He'll be with us for another six months. Winter may be hard on him."

"A doctor visits here?"

"Dr. Theobold comes once a week. More often if I send him a message," said Holbrook. "I do what I can for those here between the doctor's visits."

Jake looked at him. "I imagined a jailer would be . . . tougher . . . with the prisoners."

"I can be that," agreed Holbrook as they climbed the stone steps to the second floor. "Depends on the prisoners. Those we've got now aren't the violent sort likely to knife me in my bed, even if they had the chance. You'll see. Jails are used to store people who aren't welcome in the community. Only some are dangerous."

The second floor was much like the first, with six more cells, but it was slightly warmer. "I'm thinking to move Thomas Wilson up here," Holbrook shared. "Less dampness than on the first floor."

There were two prisoners on the second floor: David Douglas, age twenty-two, confined for six months on larceny charges for stealing small items from a mercantile store where he worked in Litchfield. And Westley Barter, age twenty-one, from Nobleboro. The courthouse and jail for all of Lincoln County were in Wiscasset.

"Westley Barter's a sad case," said Mr. Holbrook. "Martha Clarke, the young woman he was smitten with, gave birth, and in the birthing the midwife asked her who the baby's father was, as is the law. She swore the father to be Westley, and he hasn't denied it. But as the responsible man, he has to provide for Martha and the child. At the time the baby was born, Westley was living in the poorhouse in Nobleboro, which made the citizens of the town legally responsible for his obligations. They refused to help Martha, so Westley was sent here."

"But if he's in jail, how is he to support his child?"

"The good citizens of Nobleboro aren't concerned about that, nor about Martha and the baby. Westley is here for four months, or until he can think of a way to get money to his family." Mr. Holbrook shook his head. "Martha brought the baby here once to see him, but Nobleboro's a day's ride, and she had to talk a neighbor into bringing her. I doubt she'll be back soon."

Jake was silent. "I remember Father saying debtors went to prison in the old days."

"Those days aren't so far in the past. There are still men like Westley Barter who end up in the county's facilities." Mr. Holbrook led the way to the third floor of the jail.

There the floor and walls were of wood, not of stone. Four large rooms, two on each side, lined the center hallway. Jake looked through the barred windows opening into each room. Two rooms were empty. In the third a man was curled on a pallet and didn't move. In the fourth a man paced from one side of the room to the other, reciting nursery rhymes over and over.

"And then there are these poor souls," said Holbrook. "Charles Umberkind and David Genthner."

"What's wrong with them?" whispered Jake. "They don't look right in the head."

"That's the truth," said Mr. Holbrook. "They're lunatics. Crazy people. You never know what they'll do or say—to themselves or to each other. Who knows? Maybe their fathers were drunkards or their mothers didn't want them but they were born anyway. There's no way to know what causes insanity. Sometimes one of these people will come to their senses and can be released. Others stay here for a time and then go to the asylum up to Augusta. Be especially careful in working with these prisoners."

He followed Jake down the stairs. Jake looked past him, up to the top floor. "Who is up there?"

"No one now," said Holbrook. "That's the contagion ward, where we confine children or adults who have sicknesses. It's also used to isolate sailors who've been on a ship where there's been disease."

"How long do people have to stay there?"

"Until they die. Or until Dr. Theobold is sure they won't spread the disease to others in Wiscasset."

While Jake began toting pails of cold water from the Holbrooks' kitchen to the jail door, Mr. Holbrook let Margaret Flanders have a turn outside in the fenced areas, and while she was outside, Jake scrubbed her cell. When that cell was finished, Mr. Holbrook let Margaret back in and moved Thomas Wilson outside so Jake could clean his cell.

Scrubbing the stones on his knees, Jake realized how badly the cells stank of food, body wastes, sweat, and dirty bedding. He did his best, scouring the stones until his hands, already sore from oystering and chopping wood, were red and swollen and his knees ached.

After he'd finished the cells on the first floor, he scrubbed the hallway floors and the cells on the second floor. He emptied the wooden slop buckets into a larger bucket in the hall and, finally, when Mr.

Holbrook unlocked the door, he emptied the larger bucket into the privy behind the outbuildings.

By the time he reached home, he smelled like the jail, and he'd earned every penny Holbrook paid him.

But he had enough to buy corn for setting traps. And Nabby had tied a white piece of muslin on the apple tree they'd agreed on. Tomorrow he'd find her and learn how to catch a squirrel or a rabbit.

⋇ 21 ⋇

Mother was tired when Jake returned home that evening. During the day she'd prepared the entire wagon-load of apples he'd collected and strung the pieces on twelve long strings for drying. Jake hung the strings between beams in the loft before allowing himself to collapse into sleep. He wished the pieces of apple were bigger, so he could use the drying racks. Next year the racks would be good for squash or pumpkin or corn.

He'd only slept an hour or two when he woke to Frankie's thrashing and moaning, and Mother's soft singing. At first he lay there, allowing himself to be lulled by her voice. But then he knew he should see if he could help.

Quietly, so as not to startle Mother or Frankie, he climbed down the ladder from the loft. Mother was sitting on the floor in front of the fireplace. She'd added logs, for both heat and light, and the whale oil lamp was trimmed low on the table. Frankie, peaceful for the moment, was in her lap. Both she and Frankie were wrapped in the blue and red star-patterned quilt Mother had pieced several years before.

Mother looked up as she heard Jake. "I'm sorry we woke you. You had a long day."

"So did you," Jake answered. "Can I get you something? There's some tea left from the last Father brought." Granny McPherson might think tea an extravagance, but it was one of the few Mother indulged in now.

"Thank you, Jake. A cup of tea would taste very good."

Jake filled the kettle with water from the basin he kept full to save Mother from having to go outside to the pump. After he'd hung the kettle on the crane, he got out Mother's English china teapot with pink roses, and a matching cup and saucer that she had used when Mrs. Neal visited. Most days now they used pewter mugs. But tonight Jake wanted Mother to have her tea the way she always drank it in the past. They had given up so much. A cup of tea was a little thing that might comfort Mother.

"You strung close to two bushels of apples today, Mother."

Mother raised one of her hands to show some small cuts. "I've never cut up so many apples. But at least I felt I was doing something to help us. I took some of the pieces and stewed them in a little water, and then mashed them, and Frankie ate some too." She smiled at

Jake. "We're going to be very elegant this winter, dining on oysters and apples."

"Tomorrow I'll ask Mrs. Neal if she'll sell me some corn to bait traps," Jake said.

Jake was sure Mrs. Neal would help him, but he didn't have the patience to deal with Tom. If he were lucky, Tom would be off somewhere tomorrow. He wished he could ask Mother's advice about Tom, but she had enough to worry about.

"Mrs. Neal seemed very kind. But don't encourage her to come and visit again. Tell her I'll visit her soon."

Jake looked at her, surprised, as he poured the hot water into Mother's teapot to let it steep.

"You'll have to watch Frankie for an hour or two on one of the days you don't work at the jail. It will seem more normal if I visit Mrs. Neal the next time."

Jake nodded. "You're right. As soon as I get the traps set."

Mother's eyes filled with tears. "I'm sorry. I'm just so tired."

Jake knelt down next to her on the floor. "Your tea is ready, Mother. I'll take Frankie."

Mother nodded slowly. She unwrapped the quilt that covered them and handed Frankie to Jake, tucking the quilt around Frankie as she did so.

Frankie was lighter than most children of his age would be. Jake thought of Zeke and Violet. Frankie's weight was in his head and shoulders and arms; his body was thin and lifeless below his waist. Jake adjusted the way he held Frankie so his brother's head was higher.

Mother watched them for a moment, tears falling down her cheeks. Jake didn't know if Mother's tears were for her sons, or her husband, or herself.

"Drink your tea, Mother," said Jake. And he started to rock Frankie as Mother had, singing to him quietly.

❧ 22 ❧

When the rooster crowed that morning, Jake wanted to hide his head under the quilts. Only Mother's voice pulled him downstairs, calling him to share yesterday's bread softened in eggs and cooked in the skillet. He emptied the chamber pots, washed his hands and face at the pump, and settled himself at the table. The sun was barely up, but his work was waiting.

He smiled at Frankie and reached over to touch his head. "Good morning, little brother," he said.

Mother looked surprised but pleased, and spooned the egg and bread mixture onto their plates. Frankie opened his mouth for his share. For a moment he almost seemed to smile.

"Will you bring me more apples today?" said Mother. "If they're not picked now, they'll start falling and rotting on the ground. I'll do more peeling and coring after I've finished the washing."

"First I'll bring you water to heat," said Jake. Yesterday he'd brought water for Mrs. Holbrook to wash clouts; today that would be Mother's chore. "Then I'll bring you the apples. Just string those we can only use part of. This afternoon I'll layer the good ones with grasses in a barrel in the cellar."

"A good plan," said Mother. "I'll do what I can. I'm weary this morning."

I am too, thought Jake, *but tomorrow I have to go back to the jail.* Today every moment had to count.

First he had to go to the Neals' house for corn, and then find Nabby.

Mother read his mind. "Take a sack or two for the corn when you go to the Neals'," she said. "And remember to tell Mrs. Neal I'll stop by soon."

It was near midmorning before the chickens were fed, the apples were in the house, and Jake was on his way to the Neals' farm.

As he walked into their yard, Tom stepped out from behind a shed and stood directly in front of him.

"What're you doing on my land?"

"I've come to buy some feed corn and cobs from your parents," said Jake.

"I guess people in Boston eat the same food hogs and chickens do," Tom sneered. "Every time I see you, you're looking for food. I'm surprised you're not as big as a barn by now."

Jake moved to walk around him. "I just need to speak with your mother."

"Mother's in town," said Tom. "Your protector isn't here."

"I can protect myself," said Jake. "Will you sell me some corn, then? I brought a sack."

"At least you didn't expect Mother to give you one of our sacks this time," said Tom. He moved closer to Jake. "How much money have you got?"

"How much is the corn?"

"That depends on how much money you have."

Jake reached into his pocket and pulled out two coins. "Two cents."

"Two cents! I thought boys who came from Boston and knew Latin were rich! Not so poor they buy feed corn so they can eat with the hogs!"

Jake stood motionless, the coins held out toward Tom. "Will you sell me the corn or shall I find another farm that will take my money?" The only sign of his growing rage was the red color of his neck.

Tom lashed out and hit Jake's hand. The coins flew into the air, rolling into high grass. "Money? I don't see any money."

Jake clenched his fist and smashed it into Tom's nose.

He wasn't sure who was more surprised. But before the blood started trickling down Tom's face, Jake hit him again. Tom was bigger than he was, and the advantage of striking first would only last a moment.

Tom roared, and came at him, pushing him backward with both his arms until Jake's foot hit a rock and he stumbled and fell, Tom on top of him. They rolled over, each hitting the other on the arms and in the stomach and back. Jake felt blood on his face. He didn't know if it was his or Tom's. Then, suddenly, Tom stood up, wiping the blood from his nose and leaving Jake on the ground.

"Find another place to buy corn, city boy," said Tom. "Don't come back here. You and your kind aren't wanted in Wiscasset. The sooner you learn that, the better off you'll be." Tom stomped into his house.

Jake lay in the dirt for a minute or two, catching his breath. Then he got up, found his coins, put them in his pocket, and headed for Nabby's house.

She'd know where else he could get corn. He rubbed Tom's blood off his hand and cheek. He might be bruised, but at least he wasn't bleeding.

As he walked toward Nabby's home, Jake realized she'd never invited him there. Of course he had never invited her to visit his home either. The white cloth on the apple tree had meant they would meet, but they usually met in the evening, away from both of their houses.

He hoped she was to home. He had to see her.

But the yard surrounding her house was quiet. There was no sign of Nabby, or of Violet or Zeke. Perhaps they were inside. Jake hesitated before knocking. Nabby didn't talk about her mother, and he suspected she wouldn't welcome company.

He waited for a few minutes. Then he decided to stop by another time. Or wait for evening. Jake was about to leave when a short man walked around the side of the barn.

The man was perhaps thirty years old; his hair was sun-streaked, his skin rough, and his clothes worn and stained.

They looked at each other.

"I'm Jake Webber. A friend of Nabby's. Is she here?"

"Gone."

"Gone? Gone where?"

"With her pa to town. Violet and Zeke, too."

Nabby hadn't mentioned her father was coming home. In fact, Jake couldn't remember her mentioning him at all. But Cousin Ben had said Mr. McCord was a mariner, so her pa's ship must be back in port. "Who are you?"

"Simon. Nabby is my friend too. I'm watching things here for her."

Simon. Jake remembered Nabby telling him about her friend Simon. He was older than Jake had imagined. What would he be watching if Violet and Zeke were with Nabby? "Will she be home soon?"

Simon shook his head. "Don't know. She said to stay until she got home."

"Will you tell her I stopped in?" asked Jake. "Tell her I need to see her."

"I'll remember. Jake. I'll tell her."

❧ 23 ❧

Nabby wasn't at the oak tree that night. Her trip to town must have taken longer than she'd thought, or she was busy with her father.

The next few days went by quickly, but there were no white cloths on the apple tree. When Jake wasn't at the jail, he chopped wood and helped Mother prepare apples and pumpkins for winter.

It was Saturday again before Jake knew it. He'd worked three days for Mr. Holbrook and was getting to know the jail's routine. The work wasn't fun, but it wasn't as bad as he'd feared.

Mother made an apple pie in anticipation of Father's arrival, and pinned her hair up in a style she'd worn for Boston parties. She fussed with pretty dried grasses she'd cut in the field behind the privy, and arranged them in a vase on the table.

"Jake, put on a clean shirt," she said as he came in, carrying wood for the fireplace.

"I'll just get it dirty again," he said, looking down at

his hands and the shirt he was wearing. They were smudged with dirt from the logs, and from the ashes he'd shoveled out of the fireplace earlier.

"Clean yourself up and put another shirt on. Show your father you're glad he's come home," said Mother. "By now I'm sure he's accepted your decision to work at the jail."

Jake hoped so. He'd worked hard that week.

In a few minutes he was sitting with Mother at the table, waiting. She was holding Frankie across her lap, softly singing "London Bridge Is Falling Down." A very long time before, she had sung that song to Jake, too.

"I'll get us some fresh water," Jake said. "Father's always thirsty after his long walk."

"Maybe he'll have brought us some more tea," Mother said. "Ours is almost gone."

Jake hoped Father remembered to bring more dried beans. Mother had learned to soak them before baking them with a bit of salt pork, and they had become one of his favorite meals, especially when she added a bit of molasses. Or maybe Father would bring some cornmeal and Mother could make a pudding, or anadama bread.

"I'll ask Mr. Holbrook where I can buy feed corn," said Jake as they sat quietly. "I don't want to bother Nabby right now."

"Perhaps you could take her some apples on

Monday," said Mother. "You promised her some. It's too bad you and Tom haven't gotten along. But at least Nabby is a friend."

Jake hadn't been able to hide his bruises and the blood on his clothes after his fight with Tom, so Mother knew his relationship with Tom was not a cordial one.

"The apples are a good idea for Nabby," Jake agreed.

The afternoon was quickly fading. Father had not come yet.

Finally Mother stood. "It's time for supper and we're hungry. We should eat the apple pie. We'll save a piece for your father."

Jake nodded. Where could Father be? He'd never been this late. "Maybe he was busy at the mill and couldn't leave in time to get here before dark."

"Maybe he's been hurt at the mill," said Mother.

"If he were injured, someone would have sent word." Jake hoped that was true.

"He's probably been delayed on the road and didn't want to walk in the dark," Mother said. "He'll be here early tomorrow morning."

❋ 24 ❋

Father still hadn't arrived when Jake left Sunday morning to work at the jail.

Mother had slept badly, and her eyes were swollen.

"I wish you didn't have to work Sundays," Mother said as she sliced bread for Jake's breakfast in the dim early-morning light.

"Only once every two weeks," he reminded her. "The prisoners are there every day."

"I know." She gave him a hug before he left. "Take care of yourself."

Jake nodded.

Neither of them mentioned Father.

Jake scrubbed and cleaned and emptied slop buckets, and took meals to the prisoners. Margaret Flanders had gone home, but two men had been brought in for drinking too much and breaking a window at Whittier's Tavern Saturday night.

Mr. Holbrook let Jake go home in the mid-afternoon. "Everyone is quiet, and it's Sunday. You'll be able to spend at least some of the day with your family."

Jake ran home as fast as he could. Had Father come? Now was the time he usually left home to return to the mill. How was Mother? And Frankie? Often when Mother was upset, Frankie was upset too. Mother had been worried that morning. What if Father hadn't come home?

Jake was out of breath when he reached home and threw open the door.

Mother and Frankie were alone.

"Did you hear anything? Did Father come?"

"He didn't come," Mother said, "but Cousin Ben did. Your Father has joined a lumbering crew that's gone to the woods in western Maine."

"Why? Why didn't he tell us?"

"Father asked Cousin Ben to tell us. Cousin Ben said lumbering pays more than work at the mill. This time of year they'll mark trees. After the snow falls, they'll go back and cut them. Sledges can move the logs more easily on snow."

"Why didn't Father come to explain that himself?" *And say good-bye,* Jake thought. *And see if we needed his help with anything at home.*

"They needed another man to make up a crew leaving Friday, and he joined them. He didn't have time to let us know."

Jake sat down. His body felt heavy. "When will he be back?"

"Cousin Ben said sometimes crews stay in the woods for weeks."

"Weeks!"

"He brought us your father's earnings." Mother pointed to some coins on the table.

"Did Father send us a note?"

"No," said Mother. "But we know he's all right. And remember? He did tell us he was going to volunteer for jobs with higher wages."

"He didn't tell us he might leave Wiscasset!" said Jake.

"No. He didn't." Mother's words were calm, but her expression was not.

❈ 25 ❈

Wednesday night was cold and damp. Jake decided to bring one more armload of firewood into the house on the chance it rained by morning. Or snowed. The next day would be the first of November, and already the ground was hard with what Mr. Holbrook called "black frost," because it killed any vegetables left in the garden.

The moon was low in the sky. Jake stood and listened for the saw-whet owl whose "too-too-too-too-too" song had often lulled him to sleep.

In the night's silence he heard running feet on fallen leaves. He moved closer to the door of the house. Who could it be? Father? But Father wouldn't run.

Then the steps stopped.

"Jake? Jake!" Nabby's voice was low but insistent.

"Nabby—where are you? What are you doing here?"

She stepped out of the pine shadows into the moonlight. Her braid was partially undone, and had caught small twigs as she'd run. Her skirt had been torn by a thistle that was still stuck to it.

"You have to help."

"What is it?" Jake stepped toward her, speaking softly, as she was. Was someone chasing her? Were there problems at her home?

"It's Granny McPherson. Simon heard men and boys at the tavern saying she was a witch." Nabby took a deep breath. "They said that on All Hallows Eve witches can reach right from our world into the spirit world. They can tell the future, or bring back the past."

"Some folks believe in witches. I remember Irish fellows in Boston talking like that once. But I don't think anyone sober took them seriously."

"This was serious, Jake. The men said they were going to burn Granny's house, to remind everyone she was in league with the fires of hell."

"Are you sure?"

"Simon doesn't make up stories. They said if she were really a witch, she wouldn't burn, but her house would. They plan to go at midnight."

"If there's any chance they were in earnest, we have to stop them." Jake turned. "I'll tell Mother where we're going."

"Could you bring two lit candles?"

Jake nodded. He was back in a moment. "Is Simon coming too?"

"No. The men he overheard are the same who

make fun of him and do cruel things. He's better off watching Violet and Zeke for me." Nabby held out a pumpkin and a turnip. "I've made lanterns for us." She'd cored the vegetables and carved small windows in the front of each.

Jake stood the candles in the vegetables. "I've never seen lanterns like this."

"They're common in the country." She handed him the turnip. "It's a distance, and the way is dark." After the path got rougher and they had to slow down, she added, "Thank you for the apples. I've strung most of them for drying, but Violet begged for an apple pie first."

"There are more."

"I'm sorry not to have come sooner. I promised to show you how to trap."

"I came to see you one day. Simon said you were in town with your pa."

"Pa's left now. He went back to sea."

Jake thought of his father, who had also left.

"It's not much farther." Nabby held her pumpkin high. "Granny's house is just ahead, after the twist in the path."

"Who's there?" Granny's voice came through the door. "Who's bothering an old woman late at night?"

"It's Nabby and Jake. Please, open the door!" called Nabby. "It's important!"

The hinges groaned, and the door opened. Granny was wearing what might have been night garments, or perhaps they were just the long dresses she wore under her aprons. She pulled a knit shawl around her shoulders. "Come in if you must, both of you. The night air is hard on my old bones."

Nabby and Jake slipped inside, and Granny bolted the door shut. The room was dark, except for their vegetable lanterns and a glow on the hearth where Granny had banked her fire for the night.

"Is someone ill? What is so important that you pull me from my dreams?"

"Granny, there are men and boys in town at the tavern, saying you're a witch and talking of coming here at midnight to burn your house."

Granny sat on the bench by the hearth. "Are these the boys who call me names and throw stones when I venture to town?"

Nabby nodded. "Most likely."

"And no doubt I've helped a fair number of them through the years, when their mothers or fathers came through the woods to ask my assistance." Granny shook her head.

"Some of them are young men now, and they've been drinking. We came to warn you, and take you back with us. You could come to my house."

"And let those ruffians take a torch to my home? Not likely." Granny paused. "They're saying I'm a witch?"

"Yes."

"Then I should have magical powers, should I not?"

"Granny, we know you're not a witch. But those who are coming here may have been at the tavern for a time. They'll not be thinking straight," Nabby said.

"What can we do?" said Jake.

"Can you throw a stone, boy?"

"Yes, ma'am."

"Then I have a plan. The moon is not full, and there's no snow, so the woods are dark. Are you afraid of heights, Jake?"

Jake hesitated. "I don't think so."

"Well, know so! Take those two baskets over there."

Granny pointed her walking stick at two large baskets by the door. "There's a pile of stones in back of the house that I've dug out of the garden. Always thought I'd make a path, or a low wall around the house, but my back's too old to do it now. You fill those baskets with rocks, then lean the ladder I left by the maple tree up against the roof. Take the baskets and hide up on the roof. Stay near the chimney, where the roof is flat, and lie as low as you can."

Jake looked doubtful. "What am I going to do with stones on the roof?"

"You're going to be a vengeful God," said Granny. "You'll know when. Now, you go. Nabby and I have other preparations to make. Don't let anyone know you're on the roof."

Jake took the baskets and slowly headed for the door. "Are you sure your plan will work?"

"Get yourself off! It won't work if we're not ready!"

Jake left his lantern on the table and felt his way around the house to the back. Just as Granny had said, there were piles of stones several feet high. Maybe he and Nabby could come back in the spring and build her the path she wanted.

He started piling stones into the baskets. At first he just tossed them in, but they were making noise as they hit each other, so he started placing them more carefully. He worked silently.

What time was it? Would those men and boys really

come this far out from town to bother an old woman? *An old witch,* he thought. Maybe they really believed she was a witch.

What were she and Nabby doing inside? He heard nothing from the house.

He found the ladder and leaned it against the roof. The ground was uneven, and the ladder swayed when he stepped on the rungs, holding one of the heavy baskets of stones. Jake climbed slowly, balancing the basket with his body. When he reached the roof, he swung the basket up ahead of him and put it on the flat section Granny had told him about.

He climbed back down for the other basket. When he got back up on the roof, he pulled the ladder up behind him, hunkered down, and listened.

Voices were coming through the woods toward the house. And they were getting closer.

❧ 27 ❧

Jake felt nervous and unsteady on the roof. He watched the lantern lights moving down the winding path through the woods toward Granny's house.

What were Nabby and Granny McPherson doing? What if those men set the house on fire, with Nabby and Granny inside and him on the roof? His mind filled with images of flames and falling walls.

The lights were getting closer. So were the voices.

"If I'd known this place was so far, I'd have stayed comfortable, back at the tavern!"

"Witches always live way out so the devil can visit them and they can work their spells in secret."

"Granny McPherson's been here as long as anyone remembers. She hasn't done anyone harm, so far as I've heard."

"It's just a matter of waiting, then. Witches wait, and wait, and then they strike."

"Not if we strike first!"

Jake tried to see the men. They were standing just

below him now, in front of Granny's door. What if the men saw him? What if he fell?

The darkness hid Jake, but it also hid the faces of the men on the ground. For a moment one of the lanterns lit the face of one figure, shorter than the others, and Jake wondered if it were Tom. But Tom was too young to have been at the tavern. Nabby might have known who the men and boys were. Jake knew very few people in Wiscasset.

"Hey, Granny," called out one of the voices. "It's All Hallows Eve. You entertaining tonight?"

"Time for the devil to pay a visit," called another, deeper voice.

"What are those faces?" said another, lower voice. "Do you see those red faces in the windows? Are those devils?"

"WHO IS SPEAKING TO ME?"

A loud voice echoed through the woods.

Most of the men moved back from the house.

"ARE YOU THE ONES WHO'VE THROWN ROCKS AND HARSH WORDS?"

"It's the devil himself," one of the men whispered loudly.

"I AM THE SPIRIT OF THOSE YOU HAVE DISHONORED," said the strange voice. "YOU HAVE EARNED MY WRATH, AND I WILL RETURN YOUR GIFTS FROM ABOVE!"

A shot rang out. "Who shot that gun?" one man

yelled in anger. Jake saw the lanterns in the hands of the men below move away a bit, but no one answered. The men were looking up. At him?

Then Jake realized what they were doing. They were waiting for the gifts from above. He picked up a stone in each hand, and threw them down at the men. One after another, the way men had thrown stones at Granny.

"It's raining rocks!"

"Get out of the way!"

Jake kept the stones coming. Then another gunshot echoed loudly through the woods.

The men turned and ran, stumbling up the narrow path, heading back to town as fast as they could manage. Jake kept throwing stones until the baskets were empty and the voices faded into the distance.

He watched to make sure no one returned. Then he climbed down the ladder and crept to the front of the house.

The vegetable lanterns, each now carved with horrible faces, were shining in the two front windows. He knocked lightly. "Nabby! Granny! It's me!"

The door opened and he slipped inside.

"We did it! They left!" Nabby was grinning, and Granny was cleaning a musket.

"Did you really shoot at those men?" Jake asked.

"Shot through the side window, where no one was standing. Don't like to waste bullets on the likes of them, but it seemed the right time to remind 'em even though I live alone, I'm not defenseless."

"And wasn't the voice wonderful?" Nabby asked.

Granny held up a long horn. "This hunting horn belonged to my father. He could call a moose with it, or a herd of deer." She lowered her voice as she spoke through the horn and Jake recognized the deep voice they'd all heard. "It seems to drive people away rather than call them, don't you think?"

"It called down a rain of stones, for sure," said Jake, grinning.

"You young folks are welcome to visit anytime," said Granny. "Although a little earlier in the day would be more pleasant."

In the relief of the moment Jake looked at all the herbs hung from the beams, and blurted, "Nabby said you had cures. Do you have one that works for fits?"

❧ 28 ❧

"I've been so worried," said Mother, standing up from the table as soon as Jake opened the door. Washington Irving's *The Legend of Sleepy Hollow* was open in front of her, next to the pocket watch that had been her father's. "Where have you been? It's near one in the morning."

"I'm fine, and Nabby's friend is safe," said Jake. "I hoped you'd be sleeping."

"How can I sleep when my son has raced out into the night to assist someone I don't even know?" said Mother. "What would your father have said if he were here? I was so afraid something would happen to you." She went over and hugged him, holding him a bit tighter than usual.

"I'm sorry you were scared," Jake said. "I had to help Nabby and Granny McPherson. Granny's an old woman who lives by herself in the woods." He didn't tell Mother that some called Granny a witch, or that he'd climbed on her roof and thrown stones at men while Granny fired her gun into the air. Instead he changed the subject. "She knows remedies." Jake handed his mother a piece of folded red muslin. "She said these leaves would help prevent fits."

Mother dropped the packet on the table. "You told this woman about Frankie! How could you?"

"I didn't tell her. I said I knew someone who had fits and that doctors didn't know how to stop them."

"And I assume Nabby was there while you were telling Granny about this . . . friend. So now two people know!"

"Nabby won't tell anyone." Jake put his hand on Mother's shoulder. "And maybe the leaves will work. Granny didn't promise they would stop the fits, but she said they would prevent the fits getting worse, and it might make them happen less often."

Mother shook her head. "We've already tried everything. Nothing works." She picked up the red cloth packet and opened it. "Leaves." She sniffed them. "They smell like fruit. What are they?"

"She called it 'Oswego tea.' She called Frankie's fits 'the falling evil.'"

"That it is," said Mother. "An evil that came upon him with no cause."

"Granny said to soak a handful of the leaves in a quart of white wine, and then give a little to Frankie in the morning and at night."

Mother put the packet back on the table. "White wine? We have no wine in this house. And to suggest we'd give spirits to a sick child!"

"The tavern in town would have wine."

"Likely. But you're too young to buy it even if we had the money."

"I could say it was for medicine."

Mother smiled ruefully. "You'd be saying what half the customers at a tavern say. No, Jake, you will not go to the tavern and try to buy wine. They'd take you to a cell in that jail you work at, and then how could Frankie and I manage?"

"I only hoped it would help," said Jake.

Mother touched his shoulder. "I hope for a cure too." She put the packet of herbs on the shelf above her best china dishes. "We'll save the leaves, and perhaps one day we'll find a way to get some wine to see if it helps Frankie. Perhaps we could water the potion, so it wasn't strong. But don't hold out any hopes, Jake."

"Granny said it would work!"

"The other twenty or so remedies we've tried from doctors and apothecaries and herbalists were said to work too. Once, when Frankie was small, I even went to a gypsy camp where a woman was said to have cures that would take away fits." Mother shook her head. "The only thing she removed was the weight of coins in my pocket."

"This time it might be different," said Jake. "We have to try."

"Maybe when your father returns he can get us

some white wine. Until then we'll keep the leaves safe."

"Promise?" said Jake.

"I promise. And now we both need to sleep," said Mother. "Tomorrow will come sooner than we'd like."

❧ 29 ❧

Usually Jake ran to the jail in the morning and ran home again after finishing his work. Running made him feel good, and gave him more energy for the tasks to come.

But the morning after All Hallows Eve he didn't run. He was exhausted, and even the crisp November air couldn't make up for his lack of sleep. But he smiled to himself as he remembered the previous night's triumph.

Mr. Holbrook had already collected the breakfast dishes by the time Jake arrived. "Dr. Theobold sent word that a child with cholera symptoms arrived on a ship last night. You need to scrub the fourth floor rooms right away. The doctor is examining the family this morning, and will most likely bring them all here."

Cholera! Jake had heard of ships arriving from Ireland in 1832 with only a few passengers and crew left alive. Cholera killed.

There was more dust than dirt on the fourth floor;

the quarantine and sick rooms had not been occupied in the previous weeks. He turned the straw pallets over to a fresh side and made sure slop buckets were in each room.

Would he be bringing food here, and emptying the buckets? Would that mean he'd be exposed to cholera? Mother would forbid his working at the jail if she knew.

By the time he'd finished cleaning the fourth floor, Dr. Theobold had arrived.

He was a gray-haired gentleman, stooped but in command. With him were a young couple and their baby. Mr. and Mrs. Burke looked scared and exhausted. Little Erin was sleeping in her mother's arms.

"Mr. Holbrook, are the rooms ready? The Burkes need a place to rest. And perhaps you could bring them some tea?"

"The rooms are clean," said Mr. Holbrook. "Jake Webber got them ready." He lowered his voice. "How sick are these people? I have children, and you know my wife is nearing her time."

"Mr. and Mrs. Burke are fine, but little Erin is feverish and has been vomiting. Don't be concerned for your family. I think we can safely blame some bad milk she drank on her journey from New York."

"But you brought them here."

"For their safety. Not for the safety of Wiscasset's citizens. By this morning folks were riled enough to believe everyone in town was going to be dead of the cholera by tomorrow morning. These fine people are not carrying any disease. They just want to be on their way to Bangor, where they have family."

Mr. Holbrook looked puzzled. "What should we do with them?"

"Give them a place to rest for three days. It's common knowledge that cholera kills its victims within two or three days, so if they are still alive three days from now—which I don't doubt—then no one will question their leaving. I've already told people I don't believe the little girl is contagious, but I'm putting them all in quarantine to be safe."

Jake smiled at the young couple. They were only a few years older than he was, and their little girl had thick curly black hair. Mrs. Burke shyly smiled back at him.

"Some folks in Wiscasset get excited about nonsense," Dr. Theobold continued. "I heard a group of our young men got themselves liquored up last night and went out to Granny McPherson's house to make mischief. They're convinced the devil spoke to them and bruised them with stones he threw down from the sky." He shook his head. "Witches yesterday; epidemics today. It's better for the Burkes to have a safe place to stay for a few days, away from those who'd make trouble."

"Agreed, Dr. Theobold," said Mr. Holbrook.

"And could you make certain the stove on the fourth floor is lit? The baby needs warmth as well as rest. Perhaps your wife could find her a little gruel later on."

"Of course. Jake, would you show Mr. and Mrs. Burke to their room?"

Jake nodded. The way Mr. Holbrook spoke he could have been asking Jake to show them to a suite at a fine Boston inn.

As they walked up the stairs, he heard Dr. Theobold instructing Mr. Holbrook to definitely move Thomas Wilson from the lowest floor to one higher, and to give him a cough potion every three hours.

Jake went to get wood for the stove on the fourth floor, and to tell Mrs. Holbrook that tea was requested. It was good news for everyone that the Burke family did not have cholera.

❧ 30 ❧

Nabby was waiting for Jake as he passed her house on his way home from the jail.

"Thank you for going with me last night," she said. "I've smiled all day thinking about what we did."

"I have too. Even Dr. Theobold was talking about it at the jail today. He said those troublemakers must have had a lot to drink because they're telling people the devil spoke and threw stones at them!"

"As long as they leave Granny alone, I don't care what they say."

Violet and Zeke were running in circles around the house. Most of Violet's hair had come unbraided, and both she and Zeke were barefoot. Jake hoped he wouldn't outgrow his own boots. He wouldn't want to go barefoot in November.

But the two little ones didn't seem to care. "Jake! You left us apples as a surprise! Are you going to bring us more apples? Apples are my favorite." Violet tried to look coy but ended up giggling, as Zeke punched her lightly.

"I remember," said Jake. "Why don't you all bring some baskets and we'll go to the orchard and pick more before it's dark. In a few days they'll freeze, or rot on the ground. My mother's dried as many as we'll need, and I've already stored five barrels of them in our cellar."

"Can Simon come too?" asked Zeke.

"Of course. Where is he?" asked Jake.

"He's helping me layer branches around our house for winter," said Nabby. "Violet, you get the two baskets in the kitchen, and, Zeke, there are sacks we can use in the storeroom. Simon!"

"Is Simon living here now?" asked Jake.

"No. Usually by November he sleeps in the stable at the tavern and does odd jobs for people in town. He was in town yesterday when he heard the men plotting about Granny. He came to tell me, and then stayed here last night. Today he's helping me with chores. Most likely he'll return to town tonight. See," she pointed, "we've been weaving boughs of spruce and pine around the base of the house."

"Why?" asked Jake. Granny had piled branches around her house too, he remembered.

"When it snows, the branches will hold the snow and keep the winds from blowing through the clapboards. In spring we'll take the branches away, and the ground around the house will be warm and ready for the lupine and black-eyed Susans that grow there in summer. Simon!" she called again. "Come with us and pick apples. You can take some with you!"

Simon had been in back of their house. He ran toward them, as though he were a child. Bits of pine stuck to his hair and shirt. "That would be fun! Are Violet and Zeke coming too?"

"They are. They went to get us baskets and bags to put the apples in," said Nabby. "You remember Jake, don't you?"

Simon nodded. "Jake is your friend."

"That's right. He went with me last night to help Granny. You were very smart to tell me what those men were saying."

"They were saying bad things about Granny." Simon looked at the ground for a moment. "Sometimes they say bad things about me. It is hard to be brave."

"You're right," said Nabby. "Sometimes it is very hard. But you have to at least pretend. If people think you're brave, then they won't bother you."

"I try, Nabby."

"I know you do." She turned to Jake. "Was your mother pleased with Granny's cure for your friend?"

"She was doubtful, but she said the friend might try it."

"Is someone sick?" asked Simon.

Jake hesitated. Was one more person to know? "A friend of mine, Simon. Granny gave me some medicine

that might help him. But"—he turned to Nabby—
"remember? She said to add the Oswego tea leaves to
white wine. We have no wine, and even if we had
money, the tavern wouldn't sell it to me."

"You're not old enough," agreed Nabby.

"Some people drink too much. Like those bad men
last night," said Simon. "I don't drink whiskey or
wine."

"That's wise, Simon," said Nabby. Violet and Zeke
handed them each a basket or sack and then raced on,
heading for Jake's orchard. Nabby and Simon and Jake
followed them. "But if the wine would help your
friend . . . then you need it. Maybe your father could
stop at the tavern on his way home from the mill."

"Father's gone to the woods lumbering," said Jake.
"We don't know when he'll be back."

"Can wine be like medicine?" said Simon.

"Some say so," said Nabby. "Granny said when
someone has fits, then the wine was important."

"I'll save my money, and when Father is home, I'll
ask him to get the wine," said Jake. "I wish he'd come
home soon."

"Wishes are like daytime dreams," said Nabby. "If
you hope hard enough, then sometimes the way to get
your wish becomes clear."

"I have dreams," said Simon. "I dream about living
in a real house some day, like I did when I was little."

"I dream about being safe, and warm, and not having

to worry so much. And—having a red Sunday dress!" Nabby stopped. "And you, Jake?"

"I want my family together again," said Jake. "And enough money not to worry about food and fire and medicine." A year ago he would have taken those things for granted.

❧ 31 ❧

Jake was at the jail three days later when Mr. and Mrs. Burke were told they could leave.

"You're all fine," said Dr. Theobold, after checking each one of them to be sure. "I see no reason you shouldn't head on to Bangor. There's a stage this afternoon. After I check the prisoners, I'll drive you to town myself."

"We greatly appreciate your help," said Mr. Burke. "Not only in giving Erin medicine to calm her stomach, but in getting us away from those people who were so set upon our being ill. The good Lord knows, we are thankful not to have cholera. It's a horrible disease."

"It is, indeed," agreed the doctor. "We're lucky Maine has escaped for the most part so far. But with so many vessels sailing here from across the Atlantic, we won't be lucky forever."

"At least this was not the time," said Mrs. Burke, holding Erin close.

"On the chance there are people in town who still question your health, I hope you'll allow me to keep you company until the stage leaves," said Dr. Theobold.

"We would be honored," said Mr. Burke.

Dr. Theobold went down to see his other patients. Jake added enough wood to the stove to keep it burning while the doctor saw the other prisoners. "Have you come far?" he asked Mr. Burke.

"From Ireland," Mr. Burke replied. "Erin was born on the seas. I wanted to call her Atlantic, but my good wife insisted she be named after my mother, who wasn't able to make the journey."

Erin made a gurgling sound that no doubt meant she was happy not to have been named Atlantic.

"Another woman on the crossing named her son Ocean," said Mrs. Burke.

"Erin's a good name," said Jake. "I wish you well on your journey."

"Thank you. My oldest brother is in Bangor," said Mr. Burke. "He wrote that there are lumbering jobs in the north of Maine."

"My father is lumbering."

"In this great land there are so many trees there will never be an end to lumbering," said Mr. Burke. "In Ireland there were too many people, and too few possibilities. My wife and I came here to start over."

"Starting over can be difficult," said Jake.

"Nothing worthwhile is simple," said Mr. Burke.

"Jake! Come down here!"

"Pleased to talk with you. And a fair journey." Jake ran down the stairs. Sheriff Beals was talking with Mr. Holbrook in the entryway of the jail. Behind him, hands chained, was Simon.

"Hello, Jake!" Simon said. "Now I have a friend here."

"Jake, would you check to see if one of the cells on the second floor is ready? We have a new prisoner."

"Simon!" Jake blurted. "What are you doing here? Why is Simon chained?"

"Caught him stealing from Whittier's Tavern," said Sheriff Beals.

Dr. Theobold joined them. "Simon, are you all right?"

"My wrists hurt," said Simon. "And I'm hungry."

"We all know Simon. Perhaps there's been a mis-understanding," said Dr. Theobold.

"Afraid not, Dr. Theobold."

"But Simon's slept in the tavern stable for years. Sometimes they even allow him to sleep in the kitchen where it's warmer. He's never stolen anything."

"He did this time. Took a bottle of wine from the kitchen and tried to hide it under his shirt," said Sheriff Beals.

Jake gasped. A bottle of wine?

"Simon, what were you going to do with the wine?"

said Dr. Theobold. "I've never known you for a drinking man."

"I don't drink wine," Simon agreed.

"Then why did you take the bottle?"

Simon looked at Jake, and smiled. "For medicine. For a friend."

"Did someone ask you to steal the wine?" questioned Dr. Theobold.

"No one asked. I did it all myself."

Jake couldn't hold his tongue any longer. "The wine was for me, wasn't it Simon? For my friend."

Simon nodded. "For you, Jake. For a surprise. But the sheriff took it away."

The men turned to Jake. "Why was Simon getting you a bottle of wine?"

Jake had to make them understand. "It was for someone I know who's sick. Granny McPherson gave me some leaves she said I should soak in white wine, as medicine. But I didn't have any white wine to use, and Simon knew that."

Mr. Holbrook looked at him doubtfully. "You're sure the wine was for a friend? I can't have anyone working in the jail who's a drunkard."

"I don't drink! I'm only twelve!"

"Age never stopped some in this town," sniffed Sheriff Beals.

"Would you take those chains off Simon?" asked

Dr. Theobold. "Sheriff, Simon was trying to help Jake. Surely you don't need to lock him up."

"He stole a bottle of wine. He's got to do his time." Sheriff Beals unlocked the chains on Simon's wrists. "Don't you think of going anywhere, Simon. You're still in my custody."

"Yes, Sheriff." Simon shook his hands in the air to loosen their cramping from the chains.

"You know the wine wasn't yours and you shouldn't have taken it," said Sheriff Beals.

"But there were crates of wine at the tavern. They didn't need it all," Simon explained.

"It wasn't yours, Simon," said the sheriff.

"I know. And you took it away, so now I can't give it to Jake." Simon looked sadly at Jake. "I'm sorry. I tried to help."

"It wasn't his fault!" said Jake. "You're not really going to put him in jail are you?"

"Two months is the sentence for stealing," said Sheriff Beals. "I can't make exceptions, or we'd have half the town stealing wine and whatever else they wanted."

"But we all know Simon is a little slow," said Dr. Theobold.

"Simon admitted he took the wine. He knew it wasn't his. We can't excuse the feebleminded any more than we can excuse a lunatic who kills someone because the moon is full."

They were all silent.

Sheriff Beals was stern. "Simon, you're going to have to spend two months here at the jail, so you'll remember not to take what isn't yours."

Simon nodded. "I'm going to stay here. Can I have some food? I'm hungry."

"Jake, go and get that cell ready," said Mr. Holbrook. "And then ask Mrs. Holbrook for some food for our newest prisoner."

Jake swallowed hard and headed upstairs to ready Simon's cell. When he got there, he kicked the door. Hard. It wasn't fair that Simon was being punished for trying to help him. It just wasn't fair.

❧ *33* ❧

"Can Simon have visitors?" Jake asked after Sheriff Beals and Dr. Theobold had left.

"Depends on who. He's got no family around here that I know of."

"He must have had family once."

"He grew up over near the mill. Sad situation. His mother died when he was little, and his father couldn't handle a child who was slow. Simon didn't learn to talk until he was three or four."

"Where is his father now?"

"Took off for the West when Simon was six or seven, and left Simon behind. No family wanted to take in a child like that, so he grew up in the poorhouse."

"How awful," said Jake.

"Makes you wonder about a man who'd father a child like Simon and then not stay around to pay for his mistake."

"Why doesn't Simon live in the poorhouse now?"

"He's a grown man; he does chores for folks in town and earns enough to keep himself. Maybe not keep himself the way you or I would want to live, but people like him don't know any better."

Simon did know better. His dream was to live in a house.

"Could Nabby come to visit him?"

"We don't allow children to visit the jail. Not even when their ma or pa is staying here. A prison isn't any place for a child." Mr. Holbrook paused. "You work here, though, and there's no reason you can't talk to him. I suspect Simon'll be as lonely as any man in that cell."

"In jail? How can the Sheriff have put him in jail for two months?" asked Nabby. "It isn't fair. Simon doesn't see life the way other people do."

"The sheriff said he understood well enough," said Jake. "He heard that I needed a bottle of wine, and he tried to help me."

"Simon always wants to please people."

"Every time I look at him in that cell I feel guilty. If only I hadn't mentioned the wine."

"You didn't know what he'd do," said Nabby.

"Two months is a long time. He'll be there until 1839," said Jake. It was already the middle of November.

"Have you caught anything in your traps?" asked Nabby. She had explained to Jake how to set the wooden traps, and he was using the little dried corn he had left as bait.

"Two squirrels," said Jake. "It wasn't fun to clean them. But Mother made them into a tastier stew than she'd imagined."

"Stew is good, but remember to put a little salt on the meat and hang it in your chimney to smoke when you can," advised Nabby. "That way you'll have meat when snows are deep."

"Setting the traps and checking them, and then cleaning the animals, all takes so much time. How do you manage it all?"

"Someone has to. I'll be glad when Violet and Zeke can be of more help. They check the traps for me, and tell me when we've caught something, but I don't trust them with sharp knives. Perhaps in another year, when they're six."

Six, Jake thought. *Frankie is six, but he'll never use a knife.*

Though he had swallowed a bit of squirrel stew.

"I keep forgetting to ask, Nabby. Where do you get your wool for knitting? Mother would like to knit socks for winter."

"Alice Chase, who lives farther down the Alna Road, gives me her worn knitted goods, and I unravel them and knit from those. I have some yarn I haven't knit up yet. Could your mother use it?"

"She would, I'm sure. Thank you."

Nabby ran into her house and came out with two skeins of yarn, each lengths of different colored yarns knotted together. "I have another I'm going to use to knit socks for Simon. You said the jail is cold. But your mother can use these two."

Jake wondered what Mother would think of this yarn of many colors. Nevertheless, wool socks would be welcome. Every day now was colder than the one before. This morning he'd seen a spider web frozen in the corner of the privy.

❧ 34 ❧

"Simon?" Jake made sure Mr. Holbrook was occupied with one of the other prisoners before he knocked on Simon's cell door. "I got you an extra piece of bread from the kitchen." He slipped it through the little opening at the bottom of the cell door.

"Thank you, Jake. I like bread."

"Nabby can't come to see you, but she and Violet and Zeke wanted me to tell you they're thinking about you."

"I think about them, too." Jake could hear Simon chewing the bread. "I think about all the streets in Wiscasset, and the people who live there. I look through the window with the bars and I see birds. I think about what they see, and where they are flying."

Jake leaned against the cell door. "Where do you think the birds are going?"

"To special bird places. To see their friends." He paused. "I have a lot of friends."

"Yes, you do, Simon." No one had come to visit Simon.

"Do you have lots of friends too?" asked Simon.

"I have you, and Nabby. I know boys in Boston." Boys he hadn't taken the time to write to, Jake realized. How could he tell them about the life he was leading now, trapping squirrels for food and emptying slop pails from jail cells? "I'll be going to school soon. I'll meet people there. Did you ever go to school?"

"When I was little. Children laughed at me. They were nice when I helped them do their chores, but at school they made fun of me and pushed me down in the mud. So I didn't go to school anymore."

"That's sad, Simon."

"But I do have a friend here, Jake."

"You have me."

"Another friend. At night the moon is my friend. He was my friend when I was little, like Violet and Zeke. He always listens to me. And he never laughs."

❧ 35 ❧

Jake and Mr. Holbrook were the first ones at school on opening day, November 26. Jake had cleaned the small yellow schoolhouse and brought a burning firebrand from the kitchen at the jail to start a fire in the stove. The room was cold and drafty, despite the heat from the stove, and Mr. Holbrook had arranged the desks so they were as close as possible to the fire. "We don't want the ink freezing this early in the session," he said to Jake.

At first Jake had been embarrassed to wear the thick multicolored socks his mother had knit for him, but now he was glad of their warmth. He pulled his trousers down so they covered most of the colors. He'd remember to wear a heavier wool shirt under his vest and jacket the second day of school.

Students began to gather outside. When the fire was burning well enough, Jake joined them. There were eight school districts in Wiscasset, and this was one of the smaller ones, with only about sixty students. Of course, some students attended the academies and private schools in the village itself too.

He watched for Nabby and Violet and Zeke, but they weren't among those who'd arrived. Several four- and five-year-olds were clearly at school for the first time. One boy was sucking his fingers through wool mittens. A small girl with red hair held tightly to her older brother's hand. Another little girl in pigtails strutted about the school yard, showing off her new hair ribbons and blue checked blouse.

Tom arrived with Ed, who had slept in rather than come to school early with his father and Jake.

Three other boys about Tom's age joined them, and the group strolled over to where Jake was standing.

To his surprise Tom clapped him on the back as though he were greeting an old friend. "Good to see you, Jake. Boys, this is Jake Webber. He's from Boston, but he's a regular fellow. A good runner, too. I see him run by our farm a couple of times a day."

Jake waited for Tom to point out he was running back and forth to his job at the jail, but he didn't.

"Jake, you know Ed Holbrook. These other handsome gents are Jon Chase, Fred Pendleton, and Ben Tarbox."

"Pleased to meet you," said Jake. He waited for Tom to make one of his scornful remarks.

But Tom just talked with the other boys, who clearly knew each other well. They'd probably always lived in Wiscasset. Jake listened quietly as they shared local news and gossip.

"Weather was good for haying this fall; we've got a barn full, and it seems dry. No sign of rot."

"My sister Nellie is keeping company with Willis Brewer. Ma's not pleased, but Pa likes Willis."

"Did you hear—Simple Simon was arrested for stealing wine from Whittier's? Never thought he was smart enough to steal anything."

Jake's fingernails ground into his fist when Simon's name was mentioned, but he didn't say anything. The boys were right. Simon had been arrested.

When Mr. Holbrook rang the bell, they all went into the schoolhouse together. Tom and his friends might not be so bad after all.

❈ 36 ❈

"It was good of Mr. Holbrook to give you Thanksgiving day off, Jake," Mother said as she added a rabbit Jake had caught to the stew. She'd been cooking Thanksgiving dinner since the afternoon before and had already made an apple pie and a loaf of pumpkin bread. Her cooking skills were definitely improving. "No work, and no school. I'm so glad you'll be here all day."

Neither she nor Jake mentioned Father's absence, but they both looked at the door often throughout the day. They'd never had Thanksgiving without him. And they'd never had Thanksgiving without turkey and vegetables and pickles and an assortment of pies.

"Your stew smells like the best yet," said Jake, peeking into the iron kettle hanging over the fire.

Frankie banged his arm on his pallet, and Jake thought he saw him smile.

"Look at Frankie! He thinks it smells good too!"

Mother laughed. She reached over and tweaked Frankie's nose. "Frankie and I miss you while you're at the jail and at school. You get up so early in the morning and come home so late in the evening that I worry you don't get enough sleep." She paused for a moment. "Mr. Holbrook sounds very kind, but I do wish you were going to a more advanced school."

"Father said maybe next year. Truthfully, I don't know what I want to do in the future. I had thought about working in a bank, the way Father did, but after the last year I'm wondering if it might be better to take up a craft. Learn to do something people will always need."

"You don't have to make up your mind today." Mother picked up Frankie and rocked him. "Just keep your eyes and mind open as you learn. Education is never wasted."

"I wonder what Frankie would be like. If he weren't . . . Frankie," said Jake.

"I think about that too," said Mother. "Frankie, would you have wanted to be a banker, or a soldier, or a lawyer? Or maybe an artist?"

"I think he would have liked to be a musician. He always gets calm when you sing to him."

"He does. You're right." She moved Frankie so she could look directly into his face. "My son, the musician." She held him close.

Thanksgiving dinner was tasty and filling, but there was no word from Father.

Jake saved a piece of apple pie to take to Simon at the jail.

❧ 37 ❧

On Friday morning two days after Thanksgiving, Jake got to the schoolhouse early to start the stove, and then went out into the school yard where the other students were waiting for classes to begin.

The first snow of the season had fallen, and although it was only six inches deep, a small amount for Maine, there was enough to make snowballs. Tom and the other older boys were throwing them at the five- and six-year-olds, who ran in all directions, screaming with delight or panic, depending on whether or not they'd been hit yet.

Jake aimed his so they just missed the little ones, but Jon and Tom cheered when they landed a packed snowball on someone's head or face. Several of the smallest children were in tears. Jake was beginning to hope Mr. Holbrook would ring the school bell, when Nabby and her brother and sister walked down the hill from the road. Violet and Zeke were each wearing two pairs of the multicolored wool stockings Nabby had knit, but no boots or shoes. Their feet had to be cold and wet from the snow.

Jake raised his arm in greeting.

Tom saw the newcomers and aimed a snowball directly at Violet's face. She wasn't watching him, so she didn't dodge out of the way. The snowball hit her nose, and blood poured down her face. Violet and Zeke both started to cry. Nabby pulled a cloth from her pocket and tried to staunch the bleeding.

The school yard was silent. "Bullies!" Nabby yelled. "You think it's fun to hurt someone half your size?" She picked up some blood-stained snow, formed it into a snowball, and threw it directly at Tom. He ducked, but the ball hit the schoolhouse in back of him, narrowly missing the window.

Mr. Holbrook appeared in the doorway and Nabby's second snowball hit him in the chest. "What's going on out here?"

No one said anything.

"Nabby McCord, come here," Mr. Holbrook said sternly.

Nabby walked to him, looking angrily at the boys who had started it all. "Tom Neal hit my sister in the nose with a snowball."

Violet's nose was still dripping blood. "Take her inside and get her cleaned up, Nabby. Boys will be boys. You need to teach your sister to stay away from them if she can't take care of herself." Mr. Holbrook looked at everyone in the school yard, especially the older boys. "And I won't have anyone throwing snowballs at the schoolhouse, or at me. Do you all hear?"

The school yard was silent, with a few nods.

"If one of these windows broke, we'd all have to spend the winter term with snow blowing into the classroom."

He looked around. "Jake, put some more wood on the fire. Everyone else, come inside and get settled down. School is in session."

"Hey, Tom! Great throw!" Ed whispered loudly as he passed the others on his way in. "You showed those dumb McCord kids."

Jake looked over at Nabby, but she was still staunching the blood from Violet's nose. When he managed to catch her eye, Nabby looked away. Could he have done anything to stop Tom? Probably not. But he wished Nabby hadn't seen him with the others who were making trouble.

By the nooning break Violet's nose had stopped bleeding, but it was still red.

"Are you going home for dinner?" Nabby asked Jake as he added enough wood to the stove to keep the classroom from cooling off while they were gone. "You could walk with us as far as our house." Most of the children went home at noon; no one lived more than two or three miles from the school. School would resume at two, and then end for the day at four. At this time of year students who lived a distance would be walking home in the dark after school.

Jake was about to agree to walk with them, when Tom moved between Nabby and Jake. "Jake has more interesting things to do than protect little girls." He then turned his back to Nabby. "Jon and Fred and I are thinking of starting a running club for boys. We could practice in Fred's barn during the winter. His pa decided not to grow wheat this year, so their barn is empty."

Tom gradually moved Jake away from the stove, and Nabby, and toward the door. "We'd like to have four people in the club. It would be private, of course, but you're the one we've chosen to join us. You will, won't you?"

A club for running! Jake had dreamed of being friends with boys who shared his joy of running. "I'd like that, Tom. Thank you for asking me. When will the club meet?"

Jake was halfway home, still listening to Tom's plans, when he realized he'd left Nabby behind.

After he gulped down dinner at home, he ran back toward the school, hoping to see Nabby along the way. But the McCords didn't go back to school after the nooning.

Jake worked at the jail both Saturday and Sunday, doing the work he had no time for during school days, even though he worked at the jail both before and after classes. Just keeping all four stoves in the jail burning well was a full-time job in winter, but cells still needed to be cleaned, and of course there were chores at home, too. He couldn't let Mother and Frankie run out of wood. Jake passed Nabby's house each morning and evening in the dark, but he didn't see her, and there wasn't time to stop.

He'd been foolish to listen to Tom's plan about a running club instead of walking with Nabby. Tom hadn't been his friend all fall. Nabby had.

Sunday afternoon Mr. Holbrook suggested, "From now on why don't you take your noontime dinner with Mrs. Holbrook and me at the jail during the school week? That way you can check the stoves and serve the prisoners their dinners before the afternoon session of school begins."

It was clear that Jake was going to be spending more and more hours away from home. He was no longer working every other day at the jail. He was working every day at the jail, and every school day at the school-house, too.

❧ 38 ❧

Monday, December third, a nor'easter was blowing. It had snowed heavily since early Sunday night, and the blowing snow had drifted high. In some places the road was hidden; in others, it was nearly bare. Snow blew down Jake's collar and up his sleeves despite his scarf and hat and mittens. No doubt many students would be kept to home today by families concerned they'd lose their way in the whiteness.

Jake's feet were cold, his face was cold, and there was hardly any feeling left in his hands.

It took him twice as long as usual to get the fire started in the stove at the schoolhouse. The building had been empty all weekend, and winds blew down the chimney, keeping the heated air from rising.

The students who had come to school wore their coats and mittens during classes that morning. Some had brought hot bricks from home wrapped in blankets to put under their feet. Others stamped on the floor to keep their toes from freezing. Jake wrestled with the stove. Finally he gave up.

"Mr. Holbrook, the winds have blown the fire out."

There was a groan from the classroom.

"I'm cold," chattered Susan Weeks. "I want to go home."

Mr. Holbrook handed Jake the small metal box they used to carry the firebrand and hot embers from one building to start a fire in another. "Go back to the house and get more fire from the kitchen stove. Be as quick as you can."

Jake headed back to the jail and house. The winds had let up, and less snow was falling. At least now it was easier to see the road.

Jake smelled the wood smoke from the jail chimneys as he approached the building. "Those stoves have kept lit with no problems," he thought to himself. But they'd been burning all night. He hadn't had to start the fires in a cold box.

Even so, the smell of wood smoke seemed stronger than usual.

As Jake came around the corner and headed up the familiar hill to the jail, he saw why. The wooden roof over both the jail and the jailer's house was in flames.

Jake ran into the house filled with smoke.

"Mrs. Holbrook! Mrs. Holbrook!" Neither she nor the two little girls were on the first floor. He ran up the stairs. He'd never been in the Holbrooks' private rooms before.

The second-floor rooms were filled with dark smoke from the roof. Flames filled one bedroom. Mrs. Holbrook was lying on the floor near the stairs next to little Margaret. Annie sat on the floor, crying and gasping for breath.

"Mrs. Holbrook, get up! You have to get out." Jake picked up both Margaret and Annie, and ran down the stairs with them.

Annie coughed as he put her far out in the yard and gave her the baby. "Stay here, Annie. Don't go anywhere, and take care of Margaret."

The little girl nodded numbly and stood, coughing and holding her screaming sister.

Jake ran back into the house. Already the flames had reached farther, and the smoke was darker. He pulled Mrs. Holbrook up and half-dragged and half-carried her heavy body down the stairs. All he could think about was getting her out of the building. The roof could fall in at any time. Jake tried to balance himself and her body on the narrow steep steps as he reached the first floor. He'd left the main door open. The draft from the door was fanning the flames above, but it was also pulling some fresh air in to the first floor.

He staggered into the yard, holding Mrs. Holbrook. She coughed, shivered, and woke up a little as she breathed the cold air. He had no time to look for blankets. There were still men in the building.

He needed help.

Annie stood holding Margaret, round-eyed but aware.

"Annie, do you know how to get to the school?"

She nodded.

"Run there as fast as you can and get your pa." Thank goodness the wind had died down. The fire wouldn't spread as fast. It had probably started when hot ashes blew onto the wooden roof shingles.

Annie looked at her mother, who was trying to sit up in the snow. She put the baby in her mother's lap and ran.

Jake raced back into the house. He'd never touched the keys to the prison, but he knew where they were kept. He'd seen Mr. Holbrook open the doors in the prison many times, but he'd never paid attention to which key on the large ring fit which door.

He had to try three keys before he could open the door into the jail itself. Smoke was filling the jail, too, but not as quickly as it had filled the house, since the jail's roof was above the fourth floor, not the second.

He had to get to everyone. Quickly. David Douglas was now the only one on the first floor. He'd been moved there a week before. Simon, Westley Barter, and Thomas Wilson were on the second floor. And the two lunatics were on the third floor. They should be rescued first, because they were closest to the roof, but their behavior was unpredictable. Although Jake had lifted Mrs. Holbrook and gotten her outside, he knew he couldn't carry one of the men.

Besides, they were prisoners. He couldn't let them loose.

He needed help from someone he could trust.

Jake pulled two lengths of rope off the wall where they hung, inside the jail door next to the iron hand-cuffs and ankle restraints, and threw them over his shoulder. Then he wrestled with the keys, finally open-ing the door into the second floor of the prison. Smoke was already beginning to fill the corridor there. He found the key to Simon's cell. "Simon! It's Jake." The key was stiff in the lock, but it turned. Everything seemed to take much longer than it should.

"There's smoke, Jake," said Simon.

Jake opened the cell door. "There's a fire. We need to get everyone out of the jail."

Simon hesitated. "I'm supposed to stay here. Sheriff Beals said so."

"Sheriff Beals will understand. Come with me."

Jake handed Simon one rope.

Simon followed Jake to the next door. Thomas Wilson was coughing badly, his weak lungs irritated by the smoke. "Thomas," said Jake. "The roof of the jail is on fire. I'm going to get you out."

When he opened the cell door, Thomas was bent

over, coughs racking his weak body. Jake hated to bind the hands of someone so ill, but he pulled the rope off his shoulders, looped it around the prisoner's hands, and tied it. "Come on. Let's get out of here."

The two men followed Jake downstairs and through the doors he'd left unlocked. Mrs. Holbrook was now standing in the snow, trying to cover Margaret's head with her apron. Jake took the shivering Thomas through snowdrifts to a tree near the road and tied the rope around it.

"Simon, come with me. We need to get Westley and David out, and the men on the third floor."

They ran up the stairs. The second floor was still unlocked. Jake found the key to Westley's cell.

"I know what's happening. I smell the smoke," Westley said. "Just get me out of here however you can!"

Jake took the rope from Simon and quickly tied it around Westley's wrists. "Simon, take Westley outside and tie him to a tree, like we did with Thomas, and then come back and help me with the men upstairs."

Simon nodded. He had trouble keeping up with Westley as they both ran down the smoky granite stairs to the outside, but Jake wasn't worried. Westley would cooperate.

Jake took two more ropes from the hallway. On the third floor the situation would be harder. Inside the corridor the fire had already spread. Little was left of the fourth floor where Mr. and Mrs. Burke had stayed with little Erin. Thank goodness no one was there now. Jake opened the first cell on his right. Charles Umberkind was lying in the corner, under his pallet, trying to escape the smoke.

"Come on, Charles, get up," said Jake. "I'm going to get you out." The man didn't move. Jake threw the pallet off, and pulled at him. "Come on! The fire is getting closer!" Charles didn't respond. For a moment Jake thought he was dead. Then Charles started sobbing with fright.

Simon, breathing heavily from his run back up the stairs in the smoke, joined Jake.

"Charles," said Simon, kneeling next to him. "Bring your blanket. There's snow outside."

Charles looked up at him.

"And fresh air. No smoke."

Slowly Charles got up. Jake put a rope around one of his hands, and Charles clutched his blanket with the other one. "Simon, get him outside."

"Come on, Charles. We're going for a walk," said Simon. "You won't be alone. I'm going too." The two men walked steadily together through the smoke and down the stairs. Over the sound of the fire Jake could sometimes hear Simon's voice calming the other man as they made their way down to the first floor, and then out into the snow.

He opened the next door. The smoke was even

thicker here. He could barely see David Genthner backed against the far wall. As soon as David saw the open door, he raced for it. Jake threw himself across the door, and looped a rope around the man's waist. "Now we can go." Genthner jerked the rope, pulling it out of Jake's hands, and raced for the steps, the rope trailing behind him. Jake ran down the stairs but couldn't catch him. He watched as Genthner ran into the yard. He didn't have time to chase one man. Maybe the snow would slow him down.

There was still a prisoner on the lowest floor. Jake picked up one more piece of rope and fought with the iron keys again until he'd opened the door to the first floor. Here, in the lowest part of the jail, there was little smoke so far. He opened the cell that held David Douglas. "There's a fire, and I'm going to get you out of the jail. But I have to tie your hands."

"I don't need no rope," said David Douglas.

"I won't let you out without being tied. Would you rather me tie your hands, or stay in a burning jail?"

Douglas reluctantly put his hands behind his back to be tied, and he and Jake went through the iron door on the first floor and into the wooden hallway between the jailer's house and the prison, toward the outside door. Flames were now above them; smoke was everywhere, and the heat was intense. As they took a step toward the door, a section of burning roof fell down the granite jail stairs. It hit Douglas's shoulders and he sank to the floor. With his hands tied he could do little. Jake pushed the flaming wood off with his shoulder, and helped Douglas up. Together they stumbled toward the door, and threw themselves out into the snow.

Simon was waiting outside. "I'll take him," he said. He took the rope holding Douglas and helped him to a tree near the road, where he collapsed, the side of his face burned from the flames.

Jake's hair and jacket were burning. No one was near enough to help. He threw himself down in the snow and rolled over and over, pulling snow over his head and dousing the flames.

❧ 39 ❧

Someone reached down and pulled him out of the snow. Jake blinked. It was Mr. Holbrook. All the students from the school were there too. He looked around. Someone had caught Genthner, and he was now tied to a tree like the rest of the prisoners.

"How do you feel?" asked Mr. Holbrook. "The top and back of your head are burned."

"My hair caught fire, and my jacket, but I think I'm all right."

"It's a miracle," said Mr. Holbrook. "Get back, everyone," he called. "The buildings are coming down. There's nothing we can do."

They all stood near the road, students, prisoners, and the Holbrook family, and watched through the snow as the fire quickly burned the wooden house and the two top floors of the jail, destroying everything but the granite walls and stairs of the bottom two floors of the prison. The outbuildings were gone, the high stockade surrounding the exercise area was gone, and the house and everything in it was gone.

"I sent Jon Chase for Sheriff Beals and Dr. Theobold," Mr. Holbrook told Jake. "When Annie ran into the schoolhouse screaming 'The house is afire!' I didn't know what to expect." He kept his arm around his shivering wife, but no one said anything about the cold.

Simon stood near Jake. "We did it, Jake. We got everyone out."

"We did, Simon. Together, we did it."

The sheriff rode up on horseback, followed by a wagon holding members of the Wiscasset Fire Society. They arrived in time to see the last wall shudder and collapse into the snow.

Sheriff Beals went to Mr. Holbrook. "How did the fire start?"

"We don't know. Most likely ashes on the roof."

He looked at the crowd. "Did you get everyone out?"

"Everyone is out," said Mr. Holbrook, "thanks to Jake, here. He came back to light a firebrand for the school stove and found the fire. He's the one who got my family out, praise the Lord, and the prisoners."

"Without Simon I couldn't have reached everyone in time," said Jake.

"The town of Wiscasset is very appreciative," said Sheriff Beals.

"What do you want done with the prisoners?" asked one of the fire society men.

Sheriff Beals hesitated a moment. "There are six men. Correct, Mr. Holbrook?"

"Four prisoners and two insane."

Dr. Theobold joined them. "All I heard on my way through the crowd was how Jake Webber saved the Holbrook family and everyone in the jail. We owe you a great debt, Jake." He reached over and shook Jake's hand.

"Thank you, sir," said Jake. "But it wasn't only me. Simon helped too."

"Then many thanks to you, too, Simon." Dr. Theobold reached over and shook Simon's hand as well. "Now, is anyone burned? Hurt in any way?"

"Everyone inside breathed a lot of smoke," said Mr. Holbrook. "David Douglas's face was burned. And you should check Jake's head and back."

"I'll check everyone," said Dr. Theobold. "Where are you going to take the prisoners?"

"The only place I can think of is the poor farm," said Sheriff Beals. "We need a place they can be confined until another jail is built."

Simon went pale. The poor farm! The place he had grown up.

"They have little space at the poor farm," said Dr. Theobold. "Perhaps five of the men could go there. But Simon committed a minor offense, and he's served half his sentence. I'd suggest you consider his term completed. He was a hero today, and we can be proud he's a citizen of Wiscasset."

Sheriff Beals hesitated only briefly. "An excellent idea, Doctor. I can't imagine anyone objecting after Simon risked his life today. Simon, you're free to go."

Jake and Simon grinned at each other.

❈ 40 ❈

The crowd dispersed. The children went to their homes, full of the story of the big fire.

After Dr. Theobold put liniment on David Douglas's burns and determined that although Jake's hair was singed, his skin was not burned, members of the Wiscasset Fire Society took the five prisoners to the poorhouse, and Dr. Theobold loaded the Holbrook family on his wagon and took them to town to find space at an inn. With Mrs. Holbrook expecting in February, he wanted to keep an eye on her, and the safest place would be in town.

"Simon, where will you go?" asked Jake.

Simon shook his head. "Not to the poorhouse. Not to the tavern."

"Of course not." Jake hesitated. "You'll come home with me. There's space in the loft where I sleep."

Simon smiled at him. "You are my friend, Jake."

Mother turned pale when Jake walked into the house, his hair standing straight up where it had been burned, his face black with soot, and his jacket burned and covered with ashes. She jumped up. "What happened? Are you hurt?"

Then she saw Simon, who was almost as dirty as Jake. "Who is with you?" She quickly moved in front of where Frankie lay, trying to hide him from the visitor.

"This is Simon, Mother. The jail and the Holbrooks' house burned down this morning."

"Hello. I'm Simon. Are you Jake's ma?" Simon held out his hand to shake Mother's.

"Yes. I'm Mrs. Webber." She turned back to Jake. "Are you all right? What happened?"

"Mr. Holbrook sent me back to the jail to get fire for the school stove, and I saw the smoke and flames. I got Mrs. Holbrook and the girls out, and Simon helped me free the prisoners."

"So no one was hurt?"

"David Douglas, one of the prisoners, was burned a little," said Simon. "We did a good job."

"Jake? Are you really fine?" She looked from Jake to Simon and then back. "You're both covered with soot."

"That's just from the smoke, Mother," said Jake. He turned around so she could see his jacket. "My hair caught fire, and my jacket burned, but I rolled in the snow to put them out."

Mother looked at the two of them in horror.

"We're fine, Mother. Everyone is. The Holbrooks went with Dr. Theobold to find a place to stay in the village, and Sheriff Beals took the prisoners to the poor farm." He didn't mention that Simon had been one of the prisoners until less than an hour ago. "Simon had no place to go, so I told him he could stay here."

Mother nodded, taking it all in. "Then, you're welcome, Simon."

"He can sleep in the loft with me. There's space there. He won't be any trouble."

"I can help. I can carry firewood." Simon looked beyond Mother to where Frankie lay on his pallet, surrounded by other pallets and quilts. "Do you have a baby? I love babies."

Jake took a deep breath. He had never told anyone about Frankie. What would Simon's reaction be? "Frankie's my brother," said Jake. "He's not a baby. But he's not like other children."

Simon nodded, and knelt down next to Frankie. "I'm not like other people either, Frankie. But I have friends, like Jake and Nabby. You can be my friend too."

Frankie looked toward Simon almost as though he recognized him.

There were tears in Mother's eyes.

Frankie's coughing woke them all late that night. The coughs were deep and gasping, from within his chest.

By the time Simon and Jake climbed down from the loft, the coughing had sent Frankie into one of his fits. Mother held him firmly as Jake moved the quilts to protect him, and Simon added wood to the fire.

The oil lamp flickered on the table.

The fit lasted only a few minutes, and then Frankie slept. But almost every hour his coughing woke him again, and the coughing would lead to another fit. By morning he was feverish.

The snow had finally stopped. Two new feet of snow covered everything. Jake and Simon took turns using the heavy wooden shovel to dig a path to the woodpile, and to dig the wood out of the snow. They also had to dig out the door to the cold cellar, so they could get to the provisions stored there.

"Soon there will be too much snow to shovel," said Simon. "When it snows again, we will stomp the snow down and make a hard path to the woodpile on top of the drifts."

"How will we get the wood?" asked Jake.

"Dig for it," said Simon. "Like for clams."

Every time they touched Frankie's forehead, it was hotter.

"Frankie needs to see a doctor," said Jake as he tried to get his brother to swallow a spoonful of water. "His fits have never been worse, or come more often, and his fever is rising."

"I wish we could do something," Mother said. "But if we find a doctor, that will be someone else who knows about Frankie."

"If Dr. Theobold could cure the fever and coughing, then the fits might stop for a while," Jake pointed out.

"I don't want anyone to know," said Mother. She ran her hand through her long dark hair. "But we have to help him. He's getting weaker every hour."

"I've seen Dr. Theobold care for prisoners at the jail; even prisoners who were not right in their heads. He's kind, Mother, truly."

"Dr. Theobold likes me," said Simon. "He gives me medicine when I have no money. Sometimes I chop wood for him."

By noon Frankie was no better, and Mother was beginning to cough too. Simon kept the fire going while Jake bathed Frankie's forehead and hands with cool water and made Mother a cup of rose hip tea. The next time Frankie had a fit, Simon helped to hold him.

"My head is aching," Mother finally said when her coughing got worse. "And I'm dizzy. I'm going to lie down for a short while."

She fell asleep almost immediately. Mother never slept during the day, even when she'd been up all night with Frankie.

"We have no wagon or horse to take Frankie and Mother to town," said Jake. "Simon, can you walk to Wiscasset to get Dr. Theobold? Tell him Frankie and Mother are both very sick." Mother would not be pleased, but she was too weak to make a decision.

"I can do that. I will tell Dr. Theobold they are sick," said Simon.

"The snow is deep, and I have no boots your size. But Father left a coat that would be warmer than the one you have," said Jake, searching through the clothes Father had not taken to the mill. He found an elegant black wool coat, more suitable for city walking than pushing through snowdrifts. But it was longer and warmer than Simon's threadbare coat covered with soot.

"Maybe I could get some wine," Simon suggested.

"No!" said Jake. "No wine. Just bring Dr. Theobold. And soon."

If only Father were here. How could he have left them for so long? What if Mother and Frankie didn't get well?

Jake felt tears coming to his own eyes. He picked up some snow from the yard and washed his face in it. There was no time to be sorry for himself. He had Mother and Frankie to care for.

⚔ 42 ⚔

Frankie's fits continued. Jake tried to get Mother and Frankie to sip water, but they only swallowed a little. He gathered all the quilts in the house and covered them both. He kept the fire going and found the few candles left. The whale oil was low in the lamp, and in Maine it was dark shortly past four in the afternoon in December.

Both Frankie and Mother were coughing badly and their fevers were high.

It was night before Dr. Theobold got to the Webbers' home. The snow was too deep for him to use the wagon he'd taken to the jail only the day before, but with Simon's help he'd harnessed his horse to a sleigh.

Jake jumped when he heard the knock at the door. He threw open the door. "You're finally here!" He'd never been so relieved to see anyone. "Frankie's fits have been a little farther apart, but his fever is higher, and I can't get him to swallow water. Mother's in a deep sleep."

Dr. Theobold looked around the room and went to Mrs. Webber first. "We need to get her fever down," he confirmed. "Get me a basin of cool water, and the chest of medicines I left in the sleigh." Simon went for the medicines, while Jake pumped some fresh water. The water flowed slowly, and it was cold, with slivers of ice in it.

"We should wrap the pump in a rug," Simon advised as he stopped to watch Jake on his way back into the house. "If we don't, the pump will freeze, and we'll have to melt snow for water."

"We have floor coverings in the lean-to," said Jake. What would Mother think if he wrapped one of her imported woven carpets around a pump in the snow? But they couldn't risk being without pumped water. Leaving the medicines and water with Dr. Theobold, Jake and Simon wrapped the pump in the heavy wool and secured it with rope.

Jake felt himself calming down. Dr. Theobold had come. There was someone he could depend on other than himself.

Mother was confused when Dr. Theobold woke her, but she swallowed the white willow tea he held to her lips. "The tea should keep the fever down. We'll give her more in an hour. Simon, would you go and put the blanket in the sleigh over my horse? And keep the fire going. We need the room to be as hot as possible. This time of year it will never be as warm as I'd like.

Jake, take a soft cloth and keep bathing your mother's face and neck and arms with the cold water. To protect her modesty we won't bathe the rest of her body unless the fever gets even higher."

Simon piled a high stack of wood next to the fireplace so it would be available. Every time he opened the door to get another load, the winds blew in, bringing bursts of snow into the house. But the fire kept burning, and after a few trips Simon settled next to the hearth, blowing on the embers when they burned low, and adding kindling or wood when necessary.

Jake kept replacing the cool cloths on Mother's body, while Dr. Theobold went to Frankie and unwrapped the layers of quilts and cloths Jake had wound around him. "Simon, would you heat some water in the kettle?" he asked quietly as he looked at Frankie's body, and then turned to Jake. "How old is your brother?"

"Frankie's six," said Jake. He hesitated. "He's always been that way."

"Your family has cared for him well," said the doctor. "Most children born so afflicted die before their third birthdays." He took the warm water and washed Frankie and tied on a clean clout, removing the dirty one. "His fever is high, but not so high as your mother's. Does your mother have help to care for him?"

"I help some," said Jake. "But I've been working for Mr. Holbrook, and am in school."

Dr. Theobold nodded. "Your mother is exhausted as well as ill. She needs rest. Is your father living with you?"

"He's lumbering," said Jake.

"Do you know when he'll return?"

Jake shook his head.

"Is there anyone else who can help?"

"No one knows about Frankie," Jake said. "Mother and Father didn't want people here to blame them because he is crippled and feebleminded."

"Jake, I can tell that your parents are good people, because of the way they've cared for Frankie," said the doctor. "There's no reason for them to hide him. It's sad when a child is born like this, but we have no reason to believe, as our grandparents did, that such a birth is the result of sin or immorality."

"People still say it is," said Jake.

"There are ignorant people," agreed Dr. Theobold. "The truth is we don't know what causes such problems in children. Sometimes their births are early, or difficult. Sometimes an infant has a very high fever, and after that has severe fits. But in all my years of doctoring I've never seen reason to believe the behavior of the parents caused such illness."

"Can you make Frankie well?"

"I'm giving him the same white willow tea I gave your mother, but less of it, since his body is smaller," said Dr. Theobold, wrapping him again in the quilts.

"The tea should take the fever down. I also have a potion that may help his cough. Does he have trouble swallowing?"

"Yes," said Jake. "He's never been able to swallow liquids well. Mother feeds him bread or small pieces of meat or vegetables softened in milk or broth."

Dr. Theobold nodded. "Children like Frankie sometimes starve to death, or choke, because they cannot eat as normal children. Your mother was given good advice about caring for him, and has followed it well." Dr. Theobold searched through his box of medicines. "Most of the cough medicines I have would be difficult for him to swallow. But I have one potion he may be able to manage."

"Do you have anything to stop his fits?" asked Jake.

"I wish I did. But fits like Frankie's are something we still don't understand. You've kept him wrapped well, with soft pallets and quilts to prevent him from hurting himself. That, and holding him so he does not strike out, are all we can do for him."

Jake's hopes dropped. "Granny McPherson gave me some Oswego tea leaves to soak in white wine. She said they would reduce his fits."

Dr. Theobold looked from Jake to Simon. "That's why you took the bottle of wine from Whittier's Tavern, isn't it?"

"Yes," said Simon. "I thought Jake had a friend who was sick. But it was his brother."

"I don't know about the tea leaves," said Dr. Theobold. "The wine might calm the movements of the fits, but Frankie is so small even a little alcohol could slow his whole body down, and that could present other problems. I'm sure Granny McPherson meant well, and she knows herbal remedies I'm not familiar with. Indeed, I've learned a lot from her. Perhaps this Oswego tea is like lemon balm, which apothecaries sell as a cure for fits."

"Does it work?" Jake asked.

"I'm sorry to say it doesn't. There are so many diseases we know little about, Jake." Dr. Theobold was sitting Frankie up and gently spooning some of the willow tea down his throat. "We can't even control all fevers and coughs. The simplest physical problems, like cuts or headaches, can be fatal. New remedies are developed every year, but few of them work as well as we would like, and when they do work, we often don't know why. Sometimes an herb or treatment will cure one person, and not help another." The doctor sighed. "Being a doctor is frustrating. Many times we can do little to help."

Jake's mother started to shiver slightly.

"You can stop wiping her with the cold cloth, now," said Dr. Theobold. "Just cover her with the quilts and let her rest." He looked at the timepiece in his pocket. "It's almost eleven. You and Simon have both been awake and working since yesterday morning, and I don't want either of you to get sick. Both of you, go and sleep. I'll stay the night and give our patients willow tea when they need it. Do you have any rose hips?"

"Yes. Granny McPherson told me to gather them."

"That's a remedy that can work. Bring them to me, and if your mother recovers a little, I'll brew her some rose hip tea. Right now she needs the willow tea and sleep more than anything. Frankie's coughing and fits have exhausted him, too. Rest is the most important medicine for them both."

Jake suddenly realized how tired he was. And how comforting it was to have someone there he trusted, and who could help. "You'll call me if they get worse? Or if I can do anything?" he asked.

"I will. But you won't be able to help tomorrow if you don't sleep tonight."

Jake and Simon both climbed to the loft, and fell into deep sleep almost immediately.

❧ 43 ❧

Dr. Theobold's willow tea worked. By morning Mother's and Frankie's fevers had broken, and they were able to take a few spoonfuls of heated broth from the stew Mother had started two days before.

Mother was very weak. Jake helped her sit up on her pallet. She looked at Dr. Theobold. "You're the doctor Jake wanted to send for."

"I'm Dr. Theobold, Mrs. Webber. Simon came to Wiscasset to find me and bring me back."

"I told the doctor he had to come, Mrs. Webber. You and Frankie were very sick!"

"Thank you, Simon. I guess we were."

"You need rest, Mrs. Webber. You've worn yourself out caring for two boys and not for yourself."

"I care for Frankie." She smiled weakly. "Jake cares for himself, and for the rest of us, too. He's a good boy."

"He's a fine young man," said the doctor.

"He's both," agreed Mother. "I don't know what I would do without him."

"I'm going to leave some concentrated willow tea here with you," said Dr. Theobold. "Jake, make sure your mother takes two spoonfuls every four or five hours today. If her fever is not gone tomorrow, continue it then. If she gets worse, you or Simon come and get me."

"Yes, sir," said Jake.

"Mrs. Webber, I want you to take as good care of yourself as you do of Frankie. You need to sleep, and restore your strength. Swallow as much broth as you can, and rest for at least a week. Your body isn't strong, and if you don't rest you won't be able to care for your family."

"But Frankie . . ."

"Jake's been doing a fine job with his brother," said Dr. Theobold.

"I can help too," said Simon.

"Yes, you can," said Dr. Theobold.

"Doctor, how is our Frankie?" Mother's voice was still weak, and her eyes kept closing.

"Frankie's fever is down. Jake will give him willow tea if he needs it, and he has a potion for his cough. But you know Frankie is not strong, Mrs. Webber. He has already lived far longer than most children born with his afflictions, and this illness has been hard on his body. He will recover, but he'll be weaker than he was before."

Mother closed her eyes for a moment.

"You've done everything you could. And I'll be

happy to visit regularly and help when I can," said Dr. Theobold.

"We have no money."

"Many of my patients pay with wood for my stove, or vegetables for my table. You're not to worry about anything now except getting well."

"Thank you, Doctor."

"Mrs. Webber, Jake told me people have said you and your husband are the cause of Frankie's disease. I told him, and I'm telling you, that you have done nothing wrong. Sometimes a child is born who is different. We don't know why. Perhaps it is not ours to question. It's our duty to love these poor souls and care for them and give them as much life as is possible. You've done that for Frankie, I have no doubt. You mustn't blame yourself, or let anyone blame you, for the way he is."

"That's kind of you to say."

"It's not just kindness. It's truth. You've been staying here alone, just caring for your boy, haven't you?"

"Yes," Mother said softly. "It was best."

"It was not best for you. You need to be out, and visiting with neighbors. It will not make Frankie worse to go with you."

"But . . ."

"He may have fits, and some people will not be comfortable with him. But there are understanding people in this town too, Mrs. Webber. Give them a chance."

Mother was silent. "Neighbors are a far walk with a heavy child.'

Dr. Theobold looked at her. "Now you need to rest. But I am inviting your family to join me for Christmas services at the Congregational Church, and then for dinner afterward, at my home."

Mother started to shake her head.

"I am prescribing the occasion as part of your recovery. Besides, I would enjoy the company of a kind and educated woman and her family. My housekeeper is constantly complaining that since my wife died I do little entertaining."

"That is kind of you, Dr. Theobold, but—"

"I will not listen to any arguments. I will come and get you in my sleigh, and you and your family will join me Christmas Day. And should your husband not have returned by then, I can assure you that my house-keeper, Mrs. Seigars, and your sons, will be appropriate chaperones."

Jake listened. Christmas in town, with the doctor! A real dinner! And Mother out of the house. "Doctor, could I ask a favor?"

"He has already done so much, Jake," Mother said.

"What is it, Jake?"

"Could Simon come on Christmas too?"

"Of course. I'm embarrassed not to have included him in my invitation in the first place. We'll all cele-brate Christmas in good company this year."

⚔ 44 ⚔

School was cancelled for the next week so Mr. Holbrook could find a place for his family to live, and the week after that Jake and Simon remained close to the Webber home, caring for Frankie and Mother.

As Dr. Theobold had predicted, they both gained strength, but slowly. Simon helped with heavier chores, while Jake took on some of Mother's responsibilities. Simon checked their traps while Jake cared for Frankie; Jake roasted apples while Simon brought in wood. After two weeks they had fallen into a comfortable routine. No one mentioned Simon's leaving.

There was still no word from Father.

By the week before Christmas, Mother insisted it was time for Jake to go back to school.

"You've lost a week of studies already," said Mother. "No doubt Mr. Holbrook could use your help at the school, and Simon is here to help me."

"You still need to rest," Jake reminded her.

"I'll do the work," Simon said. "Mrs. Webber can tell me what to do."

So much had changed in the last two weeks. Jake no longer had a job, since the jail had burned, and he would need to find another one as soon as Mother could be left for longer periods. He had also missed school. He wanted to know how Nabby and her family were, and whether the Holbrooks were settling in to living in town.

Since coming home for nooning in this weather would be impossible, Jake packed a dinner, put on his heaviest clothes, and trudged down the road toward the schoolhouse. It had snowed almost every day so far in December. Deep drifted snow covered the road he had run twice a day earlier in the fall. Only sleighs were getting through easily, and there were few of those so far in the county. Most folks were hunkered down for winter. This far from town some tried to get to church Sundays, but most stayed home.

Jake passed where the Lincoln County Jail had stood. Piles of granite slabs and blocks that had been walls and floors were all that was left. They looked like small irregular mountains under the snow. Nabby had not exaggerated when she'd said Maine snows were deep. No snow in Boston was like this.

Someone, most likely Mr. Holbrook, had dug a path from the door of the schoolhouse to the road. The sides of the path were taller than most of the students.

In a Maine winter, drifts over seven or eight feet were not unusual. In some villages people tunneled through the snow from house to house, rather than attempting to dig the houses out.

Lessons had not yet begun for the morning. Mr. Holbrook was adding wood to the stove, and about a dozen of the older students clustered nearby, hoping to warm themselves a little. All wore heavy coats and clothing, and one girl had pulled a blanket over her head. Even with warmth from the stove there was heavy frost on the inside of the windows, and when anyone spoke, their breath was visible. No one could practice penmanship today; everyone was wearing mittens or gloves, and the ink was frozen in the inkstands.

Nabby was talking to a girl with curly red hair, whom Jake didn't know. Tom and Jon were there, and Ed was handing his father another log for the fire. They all stopped talking when Jake entered.

Mr. Holbrook closed the stove door. "Jake! Welcome back. We've missed you."

Jake crossed his fingers inside his red mittens. "Thank you. My mother and brother were ill. Simon and I have been taking care of them."

"You have a brother?" Nabby asked, stepping toward him. "I knew your mother might be ill, but you never mentioned a brother!"

Nabby must have thought the "friend" who had fits was his mother, since he'd never mentioned anyone else being at home. Before Jake had a chance to answer, Tom spoke.

"What's Simon doing with you? He's a simpleton, a fool, and a thief as well! How can you trust him with sick folks?"

"Simon helped Jake get the prisoners out of the jail," Mr. Holbrook reminded them all. "And he's a hard worker."

"Sometimes Simon helps me care for Violet and Zeke," agreed Nabby.

"None of us can do everything." Jake looked at Tom. "Some people, like you, can run fast. Some people, like Nabby, care for people. Granny McPherson and Dr. Theobold both have ways of healing folks. My father understands accounting and banking; my cousin Ben is strong and knows lumbering, and working in a mill. Mr. Holbrook managed the jail, and took care of the prisoners there, as well as teaching us." He took a deep breath, and looked at Nabby. "My brother Frankie is six years old, and he can't walk or talk, but he's taught my family patience and caring. Since he and my mother have been sick, Simon's been helping me tend to his needs, and I trust Simon to help my mother and brother when I'm not there."

Tom rolled his eyes as though he thought Jake were crazy, but the room was silent.

"Jake, we're glad you're back. My wife and I thank you every day for what you and Simon did for our family and the prisoners on the day of the fire. I hope your mother and brother are well soon."

"Thank you. I'm glad to be back at school too."

"We have only one week before Christmas," said Mr. Holbrook. "Everyone sit down and we'll see how many lessons we can cover today before the cold gets too deep for us to continue. Take your usual seats— boys on the left of the stove; girls on the right."

Jake slid onto the bench where he usually sat, and took out his slate and book.

He'd told everyone at school about Frankie. He hoped it hadn't been a mistake.

❧ 45 ❧

"Nabby! Wait for me!" She'd started for home before he'd had a chance to talk with her.

Nabby turned and smiled at his clumsy attempts to run through the snow.

"I'm sorry I paid so much attention to Tom that day. Tom and I don't have much in common but running, but I was excited about his idea of a club. Where are Violet and Zeke?"

"Pa came home for a few days, and he's with them." Nabby smiled. "The snow's pretty deep for them to walk through, and I thought it might be good if he cared for them one day, to see what I do most times."

"I suspect he'll be tired when you get home."

"He will," she agreed. "Why didn't you tell me about your brother? He's the one who has fits, isn't he?"

"Yes. My family thought we should keep Frankie a secret; that people would reject us because he is different. But most people here accept Simon for who he is. And Dr. Theobold told Mother and me that no one is to blame for the way Frankie is. Some children are just born like that." They walked slowly through the snow. Nabby's long skirts and Jake's trousers were wet and heavy.

"Family secrets are hard to keep," said Nabby.

"Yes. Dr. Theobold invited my family and Simon to attend church services with him on Christmas, and then have dinner at his home. People in town will see Frankie then, so there will be no more secrets. I thought I would start telling people now. Perhaps they won't stare as much if they know how Frankie is before they see him."

"How will you get to Wiscasset on Christmas, with all this snow?"

"Dr. Theobold is going to come for us in his sleigh."

"You're lucky. I haven't been to Christmas services in many years," said Nabby a bit wistfully.

"Maybe you can go this year," said Jake.

Nabby shook her head. "It's too far for Violet and Zeke to walk. And Pa will be at sea again by then."

"Nabby, your mother is sick, isn't she?" Jake had decided this wasn't a day for secrets.

Nabby kept walking for a few minutes; then she stopped. "Too many in town know about my family already, and you should know too. You'll hear from others soon enough if you talk with people in Wiscasset." She pressed her lips tightly together, as though trying to keep the words from escaping. "But it is shameful to tell. Ma's sick because she drinks too much. Mostly cider, but spirits, too, if she gets the chance. Not like many people do, a glass or two a day. But all the time. After Violet and Zeke were born, and Pa was at sea most of the time, it got worse. She'd forget to do the cooking, and she'd sleep so deeply she couldn't hear the babies crying. I took care of them, and got us food to eat. Now she does nothing but stay in bed. She cries more than she eats, and she sleeps more than she cries."

"Why does she do it?"

"I don't know. The minister says she is a fallen woman, and Dr. Theobold says if she doesn't stop, the alcohol will kill her. She doesn't listen."

"Where does she get money for drink?"

"Pa gives it to her. I've begged him not to, but he says she's his wife and he's providing what she needs. Then he leaves again. He says I'm old enough to manage. If I don't keep us together, then we'll all end up at the poorhouse." Nabby's voice was bitter.

"Isn't there anyone who could help you?"

"There's a group of ladies in Wiscasset who help women and children in need. I went to them once when Violet was sick and I didn't know what else to do." Nabby's face turned hard. "They wouldn't help us. They said Ma's drinking was immoral. We weren't 'the deserving poor.'"

"That's not fair!" Jake said. He thought of his

mother and father. They were struggling, but they were doing the best they could for their family. What would it be like to have parents who didn't help themselves or their children?

"Life is not always fair, Jake. You know that."

They walked a little farther.

"I'm glad Simon is living at your house now. I was worried about him. I heard about the fire, but Pa said Simon wasn't in the poorhouse. Would you mind if Simon helped me with Violet and Zeke Saturday? I'd like to go and visit Granny. To make sure she's wintering well."

"I'm sure Simon will come. Would you wish Granny the best for me? I have plans for Saturday, but perhaps the next time you visit her I could go with you."

"She'd like that," said Nabby. "So would I."

Bright sun reflecting off the snow made the world seem clean and full of light. Mother was better and planned to bake two apple pies to take to Dr. Theobold's as a contribution to the Christmas Sunday dinner. She'd already gone through the barrels of clothing they'd brought from Boston, looking for clothes she could adjust so all of them, including Simon, would be both warm and festive on Christmas.

She hadn't looked so happy and rested in a long time. Her only sorrow was that Father had still not returned. Mother didn't mention him anymore, but sometimes she stared at the door, and Jake knew she was thinking of him.

Frankie wasn't as strong as he'd been before his illness. He didn't move or cry out as often, as Dr. Theobold had predicted, and he was having fewer fits. Simon had grown fond of him, and had taken over some of his care, which allowed Mother to rest. When there was free time, Jake was teaching Simon to read basic words. He had already read Simon "The Gray Champion" and "The Ambitious Guest," his two favorite stories from *Twice-Told Tales*, and each day Simon asked if he would read more.

It was Saturday, December twenty-second. Simon had left for the McCords' to watch Zeke and Violet. The next day was Christmas Sunday.

"Mother, can you manage alone if I walk to Wiscasset? We need salt and sugar and cornmeal, and it hasn't snowed in two days. The roads are as clear as they're going to be."

"We could wait, and ask Simon to go Monday," said Ma.

"I want to see the village, and the walk will do me good," said Jake.

"I wish I could go with you," Mother agreed as she handed him the brown leather pocket that held their money. "But I'll see the town tomorrow. Frankie and I will be fine here, and you've worked hard; go and enjoy yourself. Just remember to start home early so it isn't dark by the time you return." December nights were the longest of the year; it was dark at four every afternoon, and the rooster didn't crow until seven in the morning.

It took Jake almost three hours to walk to Main Street. Some sections of the road were blocked by drifts. But close to the village the snow had been pushed down by heavy boards dragged by oxen, and was frozen hard. There the walking was not as difficult.

Jake hadn't been in the village since that morning in September when they had arrived. He had forgotten how large some of the houses were. There were streets of three- or even four-storied homes with elegantly carved doorways and large windows. Main Street in Wiscasset was nothing like Boston, but it was crowded compared with the outskirts of town where the Webbers lived.

Jake purchased what he needed at Stacy's Store, and then walked down the hill to where the Sheepscot River stretched wide and deep. Long wharves reached out to where a dozen ships, and many smaller vessels, were anchored. Pieces of ice floated on the water, but, except near the shores, the river was too deep to freeze. Jake had lived in Wiscasset for over three months, but this was the first time he'd seen the port.

Mariners of all colors, ages, and kinds of dress carried supplies back and forth from ships docked at the piers, and elegant women chatted with friends standing next to traveling bags and trunks. French, Spanish, and Portuguese were being spoken as well as English.

If he'd had more time, he would have walked down Water Street, looked into some of the shops there, and watched the ships in the harbor. But today Jake had a purpose for visiting Wiscasset that he hadn't told his mother.

The Congregational Church and the Lincoln County Courthouse towered over the village green, which was now white with snow. He turned off Main Street and headed for the corner of Washington and Federal streets. There he saw the sign: DR. PHILIP E. THEOBOLD.

He rapped at the door. A tall, muscular woman filled the doorway, an orange kerchief wound around her head and an oversize wooden spoon in her hand. "Yes?"

"I'm looking for Dr. Theobold. I'm Jake Webber."

"You and your ma are the ones coming for Christmas dinner," said the enormous woman. "Thank the good Lord, the doctor is finally letting me cook something other than the baked beans and pork he eats too much of."

She didn't move.

"Is the doctor in?"

"He is, indeed," she said. "I'm sorry. I was just so delighting in planning the dinner. You come on in."

The center hall led to a stairway to the second floor. The dining room was on one side of the hall; the parlor on the other.

"I'll let the doctor know you're here. He's in his office with a patient, so it will be a few minutes." She disappeared, leaving Jake standing in the center of the parlor. He removed his coat, put his packages in a corner, and went to look out one of the windows. He'd almost forgotten how bright rooms could be when they were lined with large windows. Glass windows this size were a luxury, and they let in cold drafts as well as light, so most smaller houses had few of them. And there were no curtains on these windows. He remembered once hearing, "Those who have no curtains have nothing to hide."

Jake heard footsteps in the hall, and turned, expecting to see Dr. Theobold.

His father stood in the doorway.

"Father! What are you doing here?" Jake started to go to him, and then realized his father's left arm was heavily bandaged and held at an odd angle. "What happened to your arm?"

"What are *you* doing here?" asked Father.

As the two stared at each other, Dr. Theobold entered the room. "I see you two have found one another. I had hoped to save that surprise until tomorrow."

No one said anything. Then Jake blurted, "How long have you been here? Mother and I have missed you so much!"

"Both of you, sit down," said Dr. Theobold. "Nathaniel's been here a little over two weeks now."

"I was lumbering, Jake, as I left word I would be. One of the trees fell at the wrong angle and crushed my arm. The men on my logging team brought me here, to Dr. Theobold."

"Why didn't you come home after that? You don't know how we've worried, and how sick Mother and Frankie were!" Jake wanted to be glad to see Father, but he was angry. How could Father have left them so suddenly? And why hadn't he come home as soon as he could?

"Dr. Theobold told me how well you were doing, and that your mother and Frankie were recovering. I didn't want you to see me as I am: a crippled failure unable to support my family in the city or the country." Father's voice was strained. "I couldn't face your mother's disappointment. Dr. Theobold said I could stay here until my arm healed."

"How bad is your arm?"

"I was able to save it," said Dr. Theobold. "But the arm will never be the same. Your father won't be able to work with the saws or logs at the mill or go lumbering."

"Can you understand why I couldn't go home, son? How could I tell your mother she had someone else to care for? A man isn't worth anything if he can't support his family."

"Mother loves *you*, not your arm. And you could still work in an office, couldn't you? You can still use your right hand?" Jake didn't want to hear excuses.

"I've talked to Mr. Stinson about doing bookkeeping at the mill. But I haven't found a job yet, and I didn't want to go home until I could feel proud to do so."

Jake shook his head. "You were wrong. We need you and love you, whether or not you have a job."

"I heard you were a hero at the jail."

"I was lucky to get there at the right time. And one of the men in the prison, Simon, helped me."

"The doctor told me how brave you were," said Father. "And how well you've cared for your mother and brother."

"They're my family. I didn't leave them."

The room was silent.

"Jake, did you come here for a reason? Is everything at home all right?" asked Dr. Theobold.

Jake turned away from his father, and faced the doctor. "Everyone is well. I came to ask you another favor." He hesitated. "Nabby McCord told me about her mother."

Dr. Theobold sighed. "She's a strong girl in a difficult situation. Her mother doesn't want to change how she is, and her children suffer for it."

"I told her you'd invited Simon and my family for Christmas. She looked so sad when she heard. Her father is at sea, and her mother would not come. But could you find space at tomorrow's dinner for Nabby and Violet and Zeke? Nabby and I could put the little ones on our laps in the sleigh, and they wouldn't eat very much. It would mean so much for them to be invited to church and dinner."

"That's an excellent plan. I would love to have all

three of them, and Mrs. Seigars will be delighted to have more people to cook for."

"Is Mrs. Seigars the woman who answered the door?"

"The very same. Thursey Seigars has worked for me for over twenty years. She makes the best soap in Wiscasset, and supplies most of the town with it. Between us, I think she makes soap because she has only me to cook for, and she has time on her hands. Women with time on their hands always find ways to fill it, and making soap is one of the better solutions, wouldn't you say?" The doctor got up. "I'll write an invitation right now that you can deliver to Nabby."

Jake started to say something, but the doctor stopped him.

"I won't tell her you talked with me. I'll just say we'll have empty spaces at our table without her and her brother and sister. You can stop and deliver the note on your way home." Dr. Theobold left the room.

"The doctor hadn't told me he'd invited all of you for Christmas dinner," said Father. "He knew I missed you all, but I was embarrassed to admit my failure."

Jake hesitated. "You didn't fail, Father. You were hurt. It wasn't your fault."

"Thank you, son. I know I haven't been the best father to you, or husband to your mother."

"We've all had hard times," Jake admitted. "You will be here tomorrow?"

"I will. And in the meantime I'll do my best to think of some way to make you and Hannah proud of me," said Father. "Please, don't tell her you saw me. I want to explain what happened myself."

"I won't tell her. I wouldn't know how to tell her anyway. But after this"—Jake stood and looked straight into his father's eyes—"there should be no more secrets in our family."

❈ 47 ❈

Christmas morning dawned bright and sunny, with no signs of more snow. When Dr. Theobold arrived at the Webbers' house with his horse and sleigh, the family was dressed warmly in their best, with extra quilts to pile around their knees and feet and to cover Frankie. At the McCords' house Nabby and Violet and Zeke joined them, giggling and snuggling under the blankets as they rode the miles to Wiscasset in style and good company.

Everyone in town seemed to be at the Congregational Church for Christmas services, and everyone in town knew Dr. Theobold. He introduced Jake and his mother to too many people for the Webbers to remember. Many of them tried to peek at Frankie, whom Mother was holding in her arms. Clearly Dr. Theobold had told at least some of them about him, and Jake saw several people shaking their heads and looking in their direction. Perhaps not everyone would accept Frankie and the Webbers. But all who were close by smiled and welcomed them.

The Holbrooks were there too. "Mr. Holbrook, I'd like you to meet my mother, and my brother Frankie," Jake said.

"It's a pleasure to meet you," said Mr. Holbrook. "Your oldest son is a very special young man. My family will never forget how he saved my wife and girls in the fire, and he and Simon saved the prisoners' lives as well."

"I'm very proud of him," Mother replied, smiling at Jake and at the Holbrooks. "And thank you for all the help you've given us. You found Jake a job at the jail, and guided him in his studies."

"I look forward to working more with him in the future," Mr. Holbrook replied. "Wherever I am, there will always be a place for Jake."

Nabby waved at two girls she knew from school, but had her hands full keeping Violet and Zeke from racing about in their excitement at seeing so many new people and places.

Dr. Theobold had brought hot bricks to warm their feet, and they all settled into the high-backed pew and being part of the first church service they'd attended in months.

Jake tried to pay attention to the words of the sermon, but his mind was on what would happen after the service, when they got to Dr. Theobold's house. He had kept his promise. He had not told Mother that Father was in Wiscasset.

Mrs. Seigars was standing at the door of the house

when they arrived, holding it open and wishing everyone welcome.

Inside, she took their outside garments and sent
all the guests into the parlor. Violet and Zeke were
the first to enter the room, and Jake heard them say,
"Oh . . . it's beautiful." When he got to the door of
the room, holding Frankie, he saw what they were
looking at.

A small pine tree was in the middle of a table by one
of the windows. Small candles, lighting up the room
with their tiny flames, were attached to the branches.
Dozens of pinecones and small red bows holding
pieces of hard sugar candy were hanging from the
boughs.

"Decorating a forest tree to celebrate the birth of
Jesus is a tradition my father brought with him from
Germany," said Dr. Theobold. "I haven't had one in
my house since my children were young, but I thought
you all might enjoy it."

"It's beautiful!" said Nabby. "Who would have
thought of bringing a tree into the house and decorating it?"

Violet tugged on Dr. Theobold's leg. "Are the can-
dies for eating?" she asked.

"Perhaps after dinner they will be." He laughed,
picking her up so she could see the tree better.

As they were admiring the tree and chattering, Jake
realized that Mother had stopped talking. She was

looking at the doorway where Father stood, smiling and watching them all.

"Nathaniel!" Mother ran over and put her arms around him. "You're here! How? And what happened to your arm?"

They stood, looking into each other's eyes.

"I'm back to stay," said Father, and they embraced again. "My arm was crushed by a tree, but I'm alive, and I'm home, where I should be."

Mother turned. "Isn't it wonderful, Jake? Your father's home!"

Jake nodded, and smiled. "I'm glad you're home, Father."

"I am too," said Father. He put his good arm around both of the boys.

"You must meet our friends," said Mother, drawing him away. "This is Simon, who is living with us now, and helping with so many things. And our neighbor Nabby McCord and her brother and sister, Zeke and Violet." She didn't let go of father's good arm as she proudly stood next to him. "Everyone, this is my husband, Nathaniel Webber."

"I have some news, my dear," Father said. "Mr. Stinson from the mill and Dr. Theobold have both recommended me for a job at the Wiscasset Custom House. My experience in Boston makes me a good candidate for it. If all goes as planned, I should be able to start work here in town in about a month, after my arm has healed."

Mother covered her mouth with delight, and then turned to Dr. Theobold to thank him for his help.

"And I have an early New Year's gift for you too." Father gestured to Dr. Theobold, and they left the room for a moment. When they returned, they were carrying a large piece of mirror. "You said that when we were settled we would get another mirror."

"Oh, Nathaniel. A mirror to fit the mahogany frame we brought from Boston!" said Mother. "It will be perfect for wherever we live." She buried her face in Father's chest as Dr. Theobold leaned the mirror against the wall, where it reflected all of them and the lights on the Christmas tree.

Father and Jake looked at each other.

"I'm very proud of you, Jake. Look at everything you've done. You've cared for our family, taken on a difficult job at the jail, proved your bravery and strength during a fire, and brought all of us together."

"I didn't do it alone," said Jake, looking around the room at Dr. Theobold and Nabby and Simon.

"We're lucky to have such friends," agreed Father.

"Finest kind," said Jake. "The very finest kind."

⊹ Historical Notes ⊹

The Panic of 1837 began when state banks that had
been given authority and funding by the federal gov-
ernment used the money to make poor investments.
Many banks failed, losing the savings of individuals and
businesses. Although President Martin Van Buren tried
to establish a national independent treasury system, the
depressed economy did not begin to recover until
1843. Many men, such as Jake's father, lost their jobs
and had to begin again.

Wiscasset was, and remains, a small seaport on the
Sheepscot River in the State of Maine, about fifty miles
north of Portland. In 1838 it was home to 2,300 people
who made their livings as farmers, mariners, and work-
ers in lumbering and other industries.

Of those 2,300 people, 983 were children who
attended one of eight district (public) schools, or one
of the private schools in the village. In 1838 New
England most children were expected to attend school
from the time they were four until they were ten or

twelve. There were two school terms each year: summer and winter, each lasting eleven or twelve weeks. The school day was from nine in the morning until four in the afternoon, with a nooning break for dinner. Boys and girls sat on benches on opposite sides of the classroom. There were no blackboards. Each student was responsible for supplying his or her own handheld slate and primer, and, for older students, quill pens, ink, and copybooks for writing. They learned by memorizing and reciting, and studied reading, arithmetic, geography, grammar, penmanship, and spelling. "Classes" were groups of students at the same level of learning, not students of the same age. Five-year-olds could be in the same class for reading as ten-year-olds.

After the age of twelve a few boys continued to study at academies or with private tutors to prepare for college. Girls from wealthier families were tutored in needlework, art, and music, or went to female boarding seminaries. But most twelve- or thirteen-year-old young adults became apprentices to craftsmen, or worked with their families at home, on farms or in family businesses.

Jake, Frankie, Nabby, Simon, Tom, and their families were not real people, but some of the people in *Finest Kind* did live in Wiscasset in 1838, and some of the story is true.

Dr. Theobold was fifty-five years old in 1838; he had been the doctor in Wiscasset for over thirty years and had outlived three wives. His son, Fred, graduated from Bowdoin College and in 1838 was married and working as a doctor in Gardner, Maine. Dr. Theobold's daughter, Ann, was also married and lived in Calais, Maine. His housekeeper, Thursey Seigars, was famous for the soap she made in large cauldrons in their kitchen.

Samuel Holbrook and his wife, Lucy, lived in Wiscasset and eventually had five children. In 1838, Samuel Holbrook was both in charge of the Lincoln County Jail and a schoolmaster in a district school. On December 3, 1838, the jailer's home and the jail did burn down, but all the prisoners were saved by school students who got them out of their cells and tied them to trees in the prison yard. The prisoners were then taken to the Wiscasset poorhouse, where they were housed until September of 1839, when a new jail was completed. The prisoners mentioned in *Finest Kind* were among those imprisoned at the jail in 1838.

The new jail was built on the same spot as the old one, and followed the same design, except that it had only three floors. Today if you visit Wiscasset during the summer, you can walk through the jail and the jailer's house, and see the granite cells that housed prisoners (in later years on a limited basis) until 1953.

Today we would call Frankie Webber's illness cerebral palsy. In the mid-nineteenth-century there were no medicines that could help him, and most people who had cerebral palsy died while they were still infants. Few lived beyond the age of two or three. At that time many people believed diseases ranging from physical disabilities like Frankie's, to mental disabilities like Simon's, to the "insanity" of some of those housed in the jail, were the result of their parents' sins. Intemperance and immorality were often cited as causes for diseases that affected the brain. Today Frankie's fits, which we would call seizures, could be controlled, and possibly stopped, by medications. Although there is still no cure for cerebral palsy, about six in every 100,000 people in the United States today are affected by it, and many live full lives.

In 1838 there was no Halloween, but Scots and Irish immigrants had brought with them traditions of fall festivals, which included fortune-telling and visiting from house to house carrying simple lanterns made from vegetables. Halloween was not celebrated as it is today until the late nineteenth century, when trick-or-treating, bobbing for apples, and predicting the future combined with black cats and carved jack-o'-lanterns to become a children's festival.

Thanksgiving was a state holiday in 1838, and the people of Maine celebrated it on Wednesday, November 28. In 1863, President Abraham Lincoln made the last Thursday in November a national Thanksgiving Day.

In 1838, Christmas in New England was still

primarily a religious holiday, celebrated on the Sunday closest to December 25. As on Thanksgiving, people attended church and then shared a special dinner. Gifts were only exchanged on New Year's Day. By the 1830s, however, some German families, like Dr. Theobold's, had begun to share their way of celebrating Christmas by decorating small tabletop evergreen trees. The "Christmas tree" gained popularity in England, and then in the United States, after Queen Victoria's husband, Prince Albert, who was German, introduced the custom to the British royal family, and others copied them.

There are no longer oysters in the Sheepscot River; they were overharvested, and then killed by water pollution. Saltwater farms in rivers like the Damariscotta are now bringing oysters back to Maine.

"Nabby" was a common nineteenth-century Maine abbreviation for the name Abigail.

And in Maine, "finest kind" is still the term used to describe the best of the very best.